"It shouldn't take us long to figure out who the baby belongs to."

"Us?" She narrowed her gaze. "What's with the 'us,' Danny?"

Her heart began to pound. She wasn't sure if it was because of his nearness or her own fear. He was so close she could smell the familiar masculine scent of him. A scent that had always represented safety, security, home. Danny. It was hard to think when he was so close.

"Danny...while you're out looking for the parents, who's going to be looking out for the baby?"

He kept looking at her until realization dawned. "Oh no." She shook her head as fear skittered over her, and raised both hands in the air as if to ward off evil. "Absolutely not."

He just grinned at her, the same grin that had been her undoing for most of her life....

Dear Reader,

Unforgettable Bride, by bestselling author Annette Broadrick, is May's VIRGIN BRIDES selection, *and* the much-requested spin-off to her DAUGHTERS OF TEXAS series. Rough, gruff rodeo star Bobby Metcalf agreed to a quickie marriage—sans honeymoon!—with virginal Casey Carmichael. But four years later, he's still a married man—one intent on being a husband to Casey in every sense....

Fabulous author Arlene James offers the month's FABULOUS FATHERS title, *Falling for a Father of Four.* Orren Ellis was a single dad to a brood of four, so hiring sweet Mattie Kincaid seemed the perfect solution. Until he found himself falling for this woman he could never have.... Stella Bagwell introduces the next generation of her bestselling TWINS ON THE DOORSTEP series. In *The Rancher's Blessed Event,* an ornery bronc rider must open his heart both to the woman who'd betrayed him…and her child yet to be born.

Who can resist a sexy, stubborn cowboy—particularly when he's your husband? Well, Taylor Cassidy tries in Anne Ha's *Long, Tall Temporary Husband.* But will she succeed? And Sharon De Vita's irresistible trio, LULLABIES AND LOVE, continues with *Baby with a Badge,* where a bachelor cop finds a baby in his patrol car…and himself in desperate need of a woman's touch! Finally, new author C.J. Hill makes her commanding debut with a title that sums it up best: *Baby Dreams and Wedding Schemes.*

Romance has everything you need from new beginnings to tried-and-true favorites. Enjoy each and every novel this month, and every month!

Warm Regards!

Joan Marlow Golan

Joan Marlow Golan
Senior Editor, Silhouette Romance

Please address questions and book requests to:
Silhouette Reader Service
U.S.: 3010 Walden Ave., P.O. Box 1325, Buffalo, NY 14269
Canadian: P.O. Box 609, Fort Erie, Ont. L2A 5X3

BABY WITH A BADGE

Sharon De Vita

Silhouette
R O M A N C E™
Published by Silhouette Books
America's Publisher of Contemporary Romance

This one's for my father.
After all these years, I still miss you, Da.
Aye, you would have been proud.

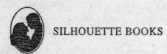

SILHOUETTE BOOKS

ISBN 0-373-19298-3

BABY WITH A BADGE

Copyright © 1998 by Sharon De Vita

This edition published by arrangement with Harlequin Books S.A.

® and TM are trademarks of Harlequin Books S.A., used under license.
Trademarks indicated with ® are registered in the United States Patent
and Trademark Office, the Canadian Trade Marks Office and in other
countries.

Printed in U.S.A.

SHARON DE VITA

is an award-winning author of numerous works of fiction and nonfiction. Her first novel won a national writing competition for Best Unpublished Romance Novel of 1985. This award-winning book, *Heavenly Match*, was subsequently published by Silhouette in 1986.

A frequent guest speaker and lecturer at conferences and seminars across the country, Sharon is currently an Adjunct Professor of Literature and Communications at a private college in the Midwest. With over one million copies of her novels in print, Sharon's professional credentials have earned her a place in *Who's Who in American Authors, Editors and Poets* as well as the *International Who's Who of Authors*. In 1987, Sharon was the proud recipient of *Romantic Times*'s Lifetime Achievement Award for Excellence in Writing.

She currently makes her home in a small suburb of Chicago, with her two college-age daughters and her teenage son.

Dear Reader,

I'm absolutely delighted about *Baby with a Badge,* the second book in my LULLABIES AND LOVE miniseries about the fabulous Sullivan Brothers—third-generation Irish cops who share a profound sense of duty, responsibility and pride in their family and their heritage. The fact that all three are gorgeous, proud, strong and stubborn is merely icing on the cake.

This miniseries is very close to my heart. Families and their intricate relationships have always fascinated me. And since I'm the mother of three, children hold a very special place in my heart and are an important part of this series, as well.

Growing up in an Irish family gave me a special appreciation for the cultural heritage each of us inherits from our ancestors, a heritage we pass on from one generation to another no matter what our cultural background or birthplace.

In LULLABIES AND LOVE we see how one family heirloom, a beautiful, hand-carved cradle, connects one generation to another through history—and love.

Baby with a Badge is the story of Detective Danny Sullivan, a man who is known for being fearless. Nothing scares Danny. A dent in his '67 Mustang might annoy him. A six-foot blonde might intrigue him. But scare him? Nothing.

Until he finds a small, squirming bundle of joy in the front seat of his unmarked squad car. The results are both hilarious and heartwarming.

In coming months you'll meet the last Sullivan brother, Patrick. I hope you grow to love these men as much as I do.

Sharon De Vita

Prologue

Dingle Peninsula
County Kerry, Ireland

He was about to lose the only woman he'd ever loved.

Desolate, he stood atop the jagged cliffs overlooking the foaming waters of Coumeenoole Strand. Night had come quickly, like an impatient lover's arms the darkness had enveloped the barren countryside in a quick, fervent caress. The foaming white capped sea rolled slowly toward shore. The soft slapping sound echoed through the darkness, playing a soft, haunting melody that matched his mood.

She would never be his.

He shook his head, unable to believe such blasphemy. But t'was to be. Today at the Puck Fair her clan had pledged her to another.

In front of his shocked eyes, he'd watched as the 'wedding matcher' had taken her hand and given it to another, sealing her fate, and dooming his.

It had broken his heart.

Bitter, he'd thought of all the plans they'd made. Since

they were wee ones they'd known they were destined for each other. She was his other half; his soul.

He'd known it the moment he'd laid eyes on her. With her fiery red hair, dancing green eyes, and lips that could make the angels sing, one glance at her and he'd lost his tender heart forever.

He knew he would never—could ever love another.

He thought of all the plans they'd made in the quiet of night when they'd snuck out to these jagged cliffs and held each other tightly, whispering of their love, their future, their sons. He thought now of the life they'd craved, the dreams they'd spun, the plans they'd made. For the future; their future.

He thought of the cradle he'd carved with such care. Intricate and beautiful, it was to be a wedding gift for his love, for the strong, strapping sons she would bless him with. Sons who would carry his name and one day have sons of their own, sons who would one day fulfill their own destiny, find their own true love.

And one day have sons of their own.

The cradle was to have been a thread from one generation to another, to be given when each had found their own true love. The cradle was to serve as a remembrance of those who had come before them, of the enormous love they'd been a part of and shared, of the memories and traditions that had been carried on by the Sullivan Clan for centuries.

Alas, it was to have been his and Molly's legacy; a precious keepsake for future generations of the clan so they would always know of their endless, enduring love.

Aye, now he knew it was for naught.

Impotently his fists clenched and he took a deep breath, letting it out slowly. Now, he wanted to toss the cradle into the foaming sea, to watch the smooth, fine wood crash and splinter against the rocks, the way his heart had been splintered.

She was never to be his.

No!

He shook his head. He couldn't bear the thought.

A cold, bitter drizzle began to fall, hiding his tears.

His heart ached for he knew there would never be another love. Not for him.

Only Molly.

Watching the foaming sea, his chin lifted; pride and anger surged through him.

He was a Sullivan, one of six brothers. They were a proud, strong clan and did not take defeat lightly. They'd been taught to fight for what was rightfully theirs. To do any less would bring shame to their name and their clan. Something no Sullivan would ever allow.

He would not sit by and let his only love slip away. Nay, he couldn't, not and live with himself. There'd be no reason for living if she wasn't his.

Molly belonged to him as surely as if they'd been tethered together at birth.

He knew it and so did she.

Defeat was not a word he could live with, nay, not and live with himself. Pride, love and his aching heart refused to accept what destiny had decided.

He could not allow her to marry another no matter what her clan dictated.

Determined now, he turned his face to the sea, letting the soft mist and the brisk wind bathe his face.

He'd been gifted with an equal amount of temper and reason. He knew he'd need both now, to think, to plan. His future—their future—depended on it, and so did the future of the Sullivan clan.

He thought of the cradle again, and determination filled him, strengthening his resolve and curling his fists.

He still had time, a chance perhaps. Molly's match was set for morn'. He still had a few hours left, and maybe just maybe…

Smiling now, he turned from the foaming sea. He knew now what he must do.

His life, their life and the destiny of the clan depended on it.

Chapter One

Nothing scared Detective Danny Sullivan of the Chicago Police Department's Gang Crime Unit.

Rumored to have nerves of steel, he had yet to encounter anything that could disturb his sense of peace and calm.

Being dateless on a Friday night might *worry* him.

Denting his mint '67 Mustang would probably *annoy* him.

A beautiful six-foot blonde might *intrigue* him.

But scare him?

Not a thing in this world.

Except perhaps for the squirming little bundle of joy he found abandoned in the front seat of his car.

In the twilight of this warm Friday evening, Danny stood in front of the driver's side door of the Mustang, scowling, not certain his eyes weren't deceiving him. He blinked, waiting for things to register.

Someone had left a baby in his car.

Scrambling for his keys, Danny quickly unlocked the driver's side door and slid in, his heart racing as he hurriedly unrolled the window further to let in some fresh air.

Seated in some kind of kid contraption, the baby was facing toward the back seat, cooing and kicking its feet, sucking on a soft, plastic toy ring, apparently pleased as punch about something.

His cop's instincts kicked in and hesitantly Danny searched the baby carrier to see if there was a note, or some sort of identification—*anything* that would give him a clue as to who this child belonged to and, more importantly, why they'd left this little tyke in *his* car.

The kid contraption had a faded yellow-and-white baby blanket tucked in and around it. Fearful of disturbing the baby, he gingerly picked up the corners of the blanket, trying to see if there were any tags or identifying marks.

Nothing.

Hands shaking, he carefully examined the child's clothing. The baby was dressed in a worn cloth diaper that was impeccably clean, thankfully dry, but obviously not new. The faded yellow T-shirt the kid had on was also spotlessly clean, but had seen better days. There were no markings or identification of any kind on either.

One tiny white sock had been kicked off and now lay on top of the front seat head rest, while the other sock remained on the kid's thrashing foot. Neither had any identifying marks.

A frayed pink bow was neatly tied to a tuft of hair that grew out of the top of the kid's head like a wild mound of strawberry crabgrass.

No clues there. Except that the kid needed a new barber.

He frowned at the baby, one large finger gently, reverently touching the pink bow. Being the great detective that he was, the fact that the ribbon was pink led him to believe the baby was a girl.

A girl baby.

In his car.

Abandoned.

Sweat broke out on his forehead, and for the first time in memory Danny Sullivan got scared.

Stumped, he stared at the baby, wondering what in the hell was going on?

Why would someone leave a baby in his car?

He shook his head.

It didn't make sense.

None at all.

Growing nervous, Danny stared at the baby much the way he would stare at a mysterious ticking package he had suddenly found in his car.

He didn't have much experience with babies. They were so little and so loud; they were the only things in the world that could scare the dickens out of him, probably because they made him feel totally…inept. Something a man with his confidence found utterly appalling.

The only child he'd had any experience with was his niece, Emma, his brother Michael's little girl. But Emma had just had her first birthday, and he didn't think bouncing her on his knee or giving her piggyback rides qualified him as much of a baby expert.

Dr. Spock he was not.

So why would someone leave a baby in *his* car?

As he looked at the baby, pain from the past flashed like a momentary beacon, but he blinked it away, willing it back to the recesses of his mind. He wasn't going to think about it. He couldn't. Not now. Not ever. It was too hard. Too painful. But staring at this little lady, so helpless, so innocent, so trusting, made it hard for him to push back the memories of another helpless baby, another baby no one had wanted.

He'd wanted it—more than anything in the world and with every fiber of his being. Rubbing a hand across his tired eyes, Danny resolutely pushed the memories away. He didn't have a choice. It was the only way he could function on a daily basis. He couldn't afford to let the memories surface now because he simply couldn't deal with them.

Instead, he focused on the most pressing problem—the squirming little infant in the front seat next to him.

Danny stared at the baby, and as if sensing his gaze, she slowly turned to look at him. For a moment, his heart seemed to slow as her beautiful baby eyes—so big, so blue, so incredibly…innocent and vulnerable—lasered in on him.

He swallowed. Hard. Pain cut him to the quick, aiming straight for his heart. God, she was so small and helpless, so…alone. Her eyes seemed to search his, watching, waiting, looking for something.

The pain he'd buried deep in his heart where no one could ever see rose slowly to the surface and he merely stared at the baby, suffused with a rush of trembling feelings he couldn't control. Lifting a shaky hand, he stroked a finger down her cheek, wondering how anyone could have just…left her. Abandoned her. It was inconceivable. Incomprehensible.

The baby waved one tiny, chubby fist in the air, then grabbed his finger trustingly, holding on as if her life depended on him.

In that instant, Danny realized it did.

His heart seemed to soften, then flip over as those wide innocent eyes tugged at him.

Devastating baby blues calmly stared at him as she clung possessively to his finger. There was such innocent trust in those eyes and that smile that Danny Sullivan, the man who feared nothing, fell hopelessly and headlong in love with a toothless little lady with a bald head and an engaging smile.

"How ya doing, sweetheart?" His voice was whisper soft and deliberately gentle.

Seemingly content, the baby gurgled, kicked her feet and grinned a wide toothless grin, clutching his finger tighter.

Mimicking her grin, Danny rubbed his thumb over her chubby fist, amazed at how soft her skin was.

"You doing okay there, sweetie?" he asked nervously, wondering if he should be doing…something. What, he hadn't a clue. "Need a drink or anything?"

The baby clutched his finger even tighter, and brought it to her mouth to suck. Danny laughed when she made a face. Her little features scrunched up as if he'd just squirted a lemon in her mouth.

"Looks like you're ready for dinner, huh?" He picked up her toy ring and handed it back to her, then looked at her curiously. "Say, little lady, think you might tell me your name? I know it's our first date and all, but introductions are sort of customary." Fascinated, he ran the back of his finger down her cheek, then over her tuft of hair, surprised at how silky it was, considering the kid looked as if she'd been trimmed with a lawn mower. "So, what did you say your name was?"

He looked at her and waited.

Big blue eyes stared right back at him, but no response seemed to be forthcoming.

"Shy, huh?" Danny rubbed his stubbled chin, his mind churning. "Well, I'm Danny. Danny Sullivan." He shook the baby's tiny, chubby fist, making her gurgle and giggle again. "It's nice to meet you. I have a feeling I'm going to be springing for dinner, but first I think we'd better figure out who you are and who you belong to."

And, more importantly, why someone had left her in his car.

For an instant, his famous Irish temper began to simmer. What the hell was wrong with people? Leaving a helpless little tyke all alone in someone's car? Anything could have happened to her.

Children were far too precious to be abandoned like a sack of groceries. It was a shame some people didn't realize that.

Puzzled, and more than a little annoyed by the apparent coldheartedness that had landed the baby in his car, Danny glanced out the window. Someone had to know something about the kid.

He'd parked right in front of the police station, just as he always did. He was, unfortunately, a creature of habit and his habits never varied. Even at this hour the area around the station was still a beehive of activity.

A fireplug had been opened, and water gushed into the street where the neighborhood kids raced through the water to cool off. Their shouts and laughter drifted through the warm air.

Cops off duty, and those who were just coming on, leaned against their cars, catching up on gossip or just having a final smoke.

Working women looking slightly frazzled hurried along the street. Still dressed in business suits and sneakers, their arms were loaded with groceries or briefcases.

A bus slowed to a halt at the corner, and the doors wheezed open, expelling a long line of weary travelers. With a belch of gray smoke, the bus was gone.

People milled around, going about their business.

No one seemed to be missing anything—especially a baby.

Danny glanced at the kid again and sighed. As a cop, he knew what he should do. He was required by law to turn over abandoned children to the Department of Children and Family Services—DCFS, as it was more commonly known.

He'd been a cop long enough to know how the system worked.

And how it *didn't* work.

The thought of turning this helpless little tyke over to DCFS or any other government agency nearly made him shudder. Oh, they would feed and clothe her, and do all that was required to sustain life. But who would hold her and comfort her? Who would nurture and love her?

Who would give her the stability and security every child needed and deserved?

He'd known the answer even before he thought of the question.

No one.

Unfortunately, none of those very basic human requirements were covered in any of the agencies' rule or procedure books. She would just get lost in the shuffle, and another innocent child would soon become just another victim of the system.

Trusting blue eyes still on him, the baby clasped her toy tight in one tiny, chubby fist. The trust in those big baby blues touched an old, empty place in his heart, and a fierce sense of love and possessiveness rose up out of nowhere, engulfing him.

And he knew then, without a doubt, there was no way he was turning this precious little bundle over to the DCFS—or anyone else who smacked of anything...official.

No way in hell.

He would find out who the kid belonged to, and then return her, but not before giving the parents an ear-blistering lecture on responsibility that they would never forget. Until then he would make sure she was properly taken care of—even if he had to do it himself.

He was a Sullivan. As such, he'd been raised with a certain amount of social responsibility. As third generation cops, he and his two brothers had learned at an early age what was expected of them. Duty, honor and responsibility to your family, your friends and your community weren't just words, but a way of life for the Sullivans.

His late father, Jock Sullivan, had instilled lifelong values in his three boys long before his own premature death in the line of duty. And turning your back on someone—especially a totally helpless, innocent child—wasn't part of the plan.

Not for a Sullivan.

Hadn't his own mother and father taken in Katie and raised her as one of their own after she'd been orphaned at five?

Danny smiled, remembering that long-ago day when Katie Wagner had arrived on the Sullivan's doorstep. Clutching his mother with one hand and a scruffy, one-eyed dog in the other, she was all spindly arms and bruised legs, with a mop of unruly red hair and big, solemn brown eyes that had immediately tugged at his heart. Dwarfing her face, they were the saddest eyes he'd ever seen.

From that moment, he and his brothers, Michael and Patrick, had accepted Katie as one of their own. She was the kid sister they'd never had. They'd loved her, protected her and tormented her as only big brothers could. She'd instantly become part of the Sullivan clan.

There had never been a question of turning Katie over to some agency. She needed them as much as they needed her.

Danny glanced down at the little lady with the silky pink bow.

As much as *she* needed *him* right now.

No, handing her over to a government agency was out of the question. His father would turn over in his grave if he ever did anything that heartless to someone so helpless. He had a responsibility, and it flowed as deeply through him as Sullivan blood.

For him, there was no choice.

As a cop, he knew what he was *supposed* to do, Danny thought with a sigh. But he'd learned a long time ago that cop or not, what he was *supposed* to do didn't always coincide with what he *had* to do—which probably accounted for the three suspensions on his record, he thought with a frown.

But he was a firm believer in the old adage that special situations required special measures.

And, boy, if this wasn't a special situation, he didn't know what was.

He grinned down at the kid. "Well, sugar, looks like it's just you and me." He picked up her errant sock and struggled to put it back on. The little scrap of material was impossibly small for his large hands. Fumbling, he tried to smooth it over her foot, but the baby kept curling her toes and giggling.

"Ticklish, huh?" Amused, he shook his head slowly. "I've got to admit, sweetie, I've always been a sucker for ticklish women." He ran a hand over her wild tuft of strawberry hair again. "And redheads," he added with a wink, giving up on trying to replace her sock. Tucking the wayward sock into the kid contraption, he frowned suddenly. "You don't need socks today, do you?" he asked, as if she would provide an answer. Just to be on the safe side, he touched her feet, making sure they were indeed warm.

They were.

Satisfied, he sighed in relief, then dragged a hand through his thick black hair, trying to figure out what to do.

He looked at the baby, but apparently she was as fresh out of ideas as he was.

Deep in thought, he stroked a hand over his stubbled cheek again. "Well, sugar, looks like what we need here is a little detective work. And it just so happens you're in luck. I am the very best detective in the Shakespeare precinct." Lowering his voice, he leaned close to whisper, "But don't tell my brothers. Michael and Patrick would only get jealous."

Giggling, the baby reached for his hand again, grabbing his finger and holding on.

The first thing he had to do was find someplace safe to stash the kid while he tried to figure out who she was and who she belonged to. It shouldn't take him more than a couple of hours to do some snooping around.

In their neighborhood everyone knew everyone—and their business—so it shouldn't be too hard to figure out who'd dumped a baby.

So what was he going to do with his surprise package in the meantime?

He *could* take the baby home to his mother, but then again, keeping a baby a secret in *his* neighborhood would be like trying to smuggle an elephant into Yankee Stadium. Nah, taking the kid home was probably not a good idea. News of his latest lady would spread faster than the flu and he couldn't afford another suspension for bucking the system and not following the rules.

Why get everyone in an uproar—especially his captain—when he was certain he would have the kid returned to her rightful owner sooner rather than later?

Tapping his fingers against the steering wheel, Danny focused on the task at hand.

What he needed was someone who loved kids and, more importantly, someone who knew that he occasionally did things the…unorthodox way and could keep their mouths shut.

Someone who wouldn't get *too* crazy about helping him look after a helpless kid for a little bit.

Danny considered for a moment, then a wide, happy grin curved his lips.

He knew just the person.

"Well, sweetie," he said as he tried to figure out how to secure the kid contraption with the seat belt. It took a few minutes and a few pithy oaths under his breath, but he finally got her fastened safely.

"Today is our lucky day." Unable to resist, he brushed his lips across the baby's forehead, surprised at the sweet, baby smell of her. "Yes, indeedy. Our lucky day."

After buckling his own seat belt, Danny started the ignition, praying Katie still had a sense of humor.

"Ms. Katie?" Four-year-old Julio tugged on her skirt. As a six-month veteran of her day-care, Julio considered himself her underboss, always on the lookout for some infraction of the rules—no matter how minor—in order to report it to her.

"Ms. Katie?" Another tug on her skirt.

"Yes, Julio?" Kneeling on the floor as she busily tended to the skinned knee of a cherubic three-year-old girl, Katie didn't bother to look up. Today was Angelina's first day of day-care and it didn't take a genius to see she was scared. After almost seven months of running Kat's Cradle, a day-care center for neighborhood children who were too young for regular school, Katie knew how important a gentle hand

and individual attention were. And this little girl with the angelic face and large solemn eyes definitely needed a gentle hand and a great deal of attention.

Two more tugs on her skirt. "Ms. Katie?" Julio waited until she looked up, his face apprehensive until he saw her smile.

"What is it, honey?" Instinctively she ran a gentle hand across his forehead, brushing the inky black hair off his face. He beamed.

"Petey's gonna feed cornflakes to Bart and Homer." Bart and Homer were their resident goldfish.

Katie smiled. "Julio, tell Petey that Bart and Homer don't like cornflakes."

"Yes, ma'am." Charged with an important task, Julio dashed off across the playroom to dispatch his message.

Satisfied one problem was taken care of, Katie went back to bandaging the little girl's skinned knee. Finished, she smiled and gently lifted the child's chin. "Angelina, honey? How does that feel?"

The child nodded solemnly. She hadn't spoken a word since she'd been brought in this morning. Experience had taught Katie that some of the children would be almost traumatized their first few days in day-care. Until they felt comfortable with her and their surroundings, she did her best to give them as much of her personal attention and love as possible.

In a week she was certain Angelina would be tearing across the room, playing with the other children, her first few frightening days forgotten.

"Ms. Katie?" Julio was back, bouncing on the balls of his feet. He tugged on her skirt again. "Ms. Katie?" Breathless, his near black eyes were wide and his face was flushed with excitement. "Petey said he's gonna dump my shoes in the toilet for tattling."

Katie swallowed a smile, as she turned her attention to Julio, who was waiting expectantly for direction. "Tell Petey that shoes don't belong in the toilet."

"Shoes don't belong in the toilet," Julio repeated, making sure he got it right. Satisfied, he grinned. "Okay."

He raced off again as Katie glanced across the room. She caught Petey's eye, noting he had Julio's beat-up sneakers in his hands, fully intending to do damage. Words weren't necessary. Petey knew the rules. Katie shook her head slowly until he nodded in acknowledgment.

At six, Petey was the oldest child in her care and the only one of school age. Petey's mother was going through a particularly difficult divorce, and currently they were staying with Petey's grandmother. Since it was a temporary situation, Petey's mother hadn't been able to register him for regular school. So Katie had bent the rules a bit and allowed Petey to stay in her care.

At the moment, Petey had enough confusion and turmoil in his life, and so did his mother. Katie certainly didn't want to add to it. Knowing Petey would feel more comfortable in friendly surroundings, she'd agreed to let him stay as long as necessary.

It wasn't the first time she'd bent the stringent rules. Kat's Cradle had been her dream for as long as she could remember, but she'd had no idea there was so much paperwork and bureaucracy necessary in order to become properly licensed as a day-care center.

She'd been interviewed, photographed and fingerprinted. A background check had been run, as well as a check with police and the FBI in order to be certain she had no criminal record in the state of Illinois or any other state.

It had taken six long cumbersome months to muddle through everything in order to get her license approved. And in all honesty the rules and regulations hadn't bothered her since she knew they had been put in place merely for the children's protection.

In the end it had been worth all the aggravation—not to mention the huge dip in her savings—to fulfill her dream and open the day-care center.

She had been up and running nearly seven months now,

a duly licensed child-care agency of the State of Illinois, as well as licensed and approved by the Department of Children and Family Services, which also required her to follow strict guidelines regarding the care of the children in her custody.

No, Petey wasn't the first child she'd bent or stretched the rules for. She simply didn't have the heart to turn away a child who needed her. Perhaps because at one time she had been a child in need and knew how it felt to be displaced from your home, your family and all that was familiar. As a result, if she could help just one child, give just one a touch of kindness, a touch of love, stability and security, it was worth the constant worry that went along with trying to follow all the rules and regulations.

"I have to go potty." The soft, scared voice belonged to Angelina, who stared up at Katie with a mixture of fear and apprehension.

Touched by the child's fear, Katie smiled, stroking a gentle hand down the little girl's beautiful long hair. "Would you like me to take you, sweetheart?"

Angelina nodded solemnly, then took Katie's outstretched hand and allowed her to lead her to the washroom.

For some reason it had been a light month. There were only four children in her care at the moment: Julio, Petey, Angelina and Bobby, a redheaded little urchin who, at almost five, was more charming and conniving than males ten times his age. But considering his past, he should be.

Bobby's parents were professional pickpockets and they'd had him plying their trade on the busy downtown streets of Chicago as soon as he was old enough to walk.

After a cop had watched Bobby relieve a visiting tourist of his wallet, the little thief-in-training had been removed from his parents' care and placed in the custody of DCFS. Unfortunately, DCFS was short of licensed and approved foster homes at the moment, so during the day Bobby stayed with her at day-care, and at night was returned to a DCFS emergency shelter.

"Start cleaning up, boys," Katie called as she guided Angelina toward the washroom.

"Come along now, children, you heard Ms. Katie." Smiling, Mrs. Hennypenny, Katie's assistant, shepherded and cajoled Julio and the others to begin cleaning up.

At sixty, Mrs. Hennypenny was an angel, and the perfect assistant. With her steel gray hair and sparkling blue eyes, she was almost as round as she was tall, with an ample lap and eager arms meant for hugging and cuddling. After twenty-five years as a public school teacher, Mrs. Hennypenny had retired, and found herself bored to death.

A widow, Mrs. Hennypenny had been left all alone when her only son moved out of state. She had sorely missed her six grandchildren and found herself with nothing to do all day. So on the day Katie opened the center, she'd stopped by and offered to donate her time as Katie's assistant.

Grateful, Katie had accepted. Within weeks, the center was so busy and Mrs. Hennypenny was so good with the children that Katie had put her on the payroll full-time. Now Katie loved her as much as the children, and had no idea what she would do without her.

"Ms. Katie?" There was a hard rapid knock-knock outside the bathroom door.

Trying not to smile, Katie helped Angelina straighten her clothes. "Yes, Julio?"

"Are we allowed to have guns?"

She shook her head, grateful the door still separated them. Julio would be unbearable if he had any idea how much she enjoyed his daily escapades. The range and strangeness of the child's endless questions were merely a testament to his innate curiosity.

"No, Julio," she said patiently. "You're not allowed to have guns. Remember the day you arrived when I explained the rules?"

She had a strict policy that no toys of a violent nature were allowed at the center. No guns. No rockets. No bows, arrows or slingshots. Nothing that could be used to hurt someone. Nothing that would promote or incite any type of violent behavior. Children could learn a whole host of things at Kat's Cradle, but violence was definitely not one of them.

"I remember," Julio said through the closed door. "No guns allowed, right?"

"Right." Suspicious, she frowned, then opened the door and peeked around it. "Julio, what made you ask me about guns?"

"'Cuz."

"'Cause...why?" she asked skeptically. He was looking particularly pleased about something. That made her nervous. Definitely.

Crossing his arms across his chest in a mannerism that was far too mature for his age, Julio grinned, revealing two missing top teeth and an adorable dimple. "'Cuz there's a man at the back door and he's got a gun."

Chapter Two

"**W**hat!" Katie's gaze flew to the back door that led to the alley. Her heart pumped into fearful overtime when she saw the tall, dark silhouette of a man in the block window. She couldn't make out the face through the curtains, just the shadow. But the small, child-size chair pulled up to the back door explained how Julio had seen the man. And his gun. The little mischief-maker had been peeking out the windows again.

"I'll go tell him you said he can't have a gun," Julio announced.

She caught him by the back of his shirt, reining him in just as he was about to race off and deliver her message to the mysterious gun-toting stranger. "No, thank you, Julio," she said, struggling to keep her voice calm. Her mind was racing and her fractured attention was on whoever was outside. "I'll handle it."

The children's safety was always her utmost concern. Even though the center was located in the heart of Logan Square, the neighborhood where she'd grown up, it was an area that was going through a great deal of change—and not for the better. Gangs were encroaching, and growing bolder in their desire to claim more "turf". Unfortunately, her center was right smack in the middle of two different gangs' turfs.

But with the 14th District Shakespeare police station just blocks away, and Michael, Danny and Patrick Sullivan all stationed at the 14th, she hadn't been too concerned, knowing that, if necessary, reinforcements were close at hand. And having grown up in the neighborhood, she wasn't afraid, but she also wasn't foolish. She'd had a few…uncomfortable moments of worry, but nothing she couldn't handle.

Then again, Katie thought with a frown, she'd never been confronted by a gun-toting stranger before.

And any man with a gun was to be considered a danger.

She thought about calling the police, but then decided she'd better check the situation out herself first. Julio was known to exaggerate, and she didn't want to alert the police unless there really was a problem.

Besides, if she phoned the station, she knew that Danny, Patrick or Michael would converge on the shelter like a hungry posse. They considered her one of their own. Even though they weren't related by blood, they were related by love, history and experiences. To the Sullivans, that was more than enough.

Family was sacred to the Sullivans. The merest hint that she or her charges might be in any kind of danger would bring out all the protective instincts of her legendary adoptive family. But at the moment, she didn't think their presence would be a benefit to her charges. Instead, the mere sight of the three large, formidable Sullivan brothers was likely to scare her little kids to death.

So before she immediately called in the reinforcements, she would see if she could handle the situation on her own. An independence she'd only begun to exercise in the past year since she'd returned home.

What a stark contrast to the little girl who'd arrived at

the Sullivans, bedraggled, frightened and with little more
than a tattered stuffed bear named Barclay. From that moment forward all three of the Sullivan brothers had taken
her under their wing and into their hearts.

But no one more so than Danny.

From the day she arrived at the Sullivan home, Danny
had considered himself her self-appointed protector. The
death of her parents had left a huge, gaping hole in her life
and in her tender, aching heart, but it was Danny who'd
done his best to fill it.

Dear, sweet, fearless Danny who was rough and tough
on the outside, but who had a heart of gold on the inside.

Not that he would ever admit it.

She wasn't quite certain when she'd fallen in love with
him. But her feelings had gone from a child's blind ado-
ration, to a teenager's naive crush, to a young woman's
first, romantic love, to the kind of enduring, encompassing
love a woman searched for her whole life.

Unfortunately, Danny still looked at her as if she were a
kid. His cute little kid sister. Ugh. Just the thought was
enough to make her want to scream, and it was one of the
reasons she'd stayed away from home for so long.

After college, she'd wisely chosen to take a job out of
state. She hadn't wanted to return home until she was either
over Danny, or until she could make him see her as something more than a little kid.

Once, when she was a gawky fourteen-year-old and
hopelessly, wildly in love with him—and quite certain she
would die, absolutely die, if she didn't tell him—she'd foolishly confessed her feelings for him. Unfortunately, she'd
chosen to do it in full view of all of his friends.

Mistake!

Unaware of how very real her feelings for him were, for
the rest of that miserable summer, Danny, as well as his
friends, had laughed and teased her about her untimely confession. Lovesick and humiliated beyond belief by Danny's
rejection, she'd vowed never again to let him know how

she truly felt about him. As Irish as the Sullivans, she knew a little bit about stubborn pride, and she would die before she ever let Danny know she was still in love with him.

True to her word, she'd never revealed her feelings for Danny again. And from that moment on, their relationship had been irrevocably changed. Gone was the closeness, the friendly camaraderie they'd once shared, and she missed it. Oh, Danny still treated her the same, at least on the surface, but she knew there was a difference. Before her ill-fated confession, they'd been close as two peas in a pod, and she'd never given up hope that one day they would be able to repair their relationship.

When she returned home a little over a year ago, she'd done so knowing she would either have to forget about Danny and get on with her life—without him. Or she was going to have to get Danny to acknowledge that she was no longer a helpless, hopeless kid—or his sister. It was about time he began seeing her as a woman. A warm, loving, desirable woman.

She just hadn't quite figured out how she was going to do that yet. But she was working on it, and hopefully she would be able to come up with something soon.

She wondered if confronting a gun-toting stranger just might do the trick.

Possibly.

On the other hand it could also get her killed.

"Julio, take Angelina to Mrs. Hennypenny and tell her to take all the children into the kitchen."

"But—"

"Go do it. *Now*, Julio," she ordered in a voice that brooked no argument. "And no more chair climbing. Understand?"

Katie smiled, giving him an affectionate pat on the shoulder. "Good. Now go."

Taking Angelina's hand, Julio dashed across the room, dragging the little girl along with him whether she wanted to go or not, obviously anxious to pass along his orders.

Smoothing her short cap of unruly auburn curls with a nervous hand, Katie took a deep breath. She looked out the window, expecting to see the intruder but saw...no one. Instantly alert, she moved Julio's chair out of the way, unlocked the double bolt with the key that was permanently in the lock for safety reasons, then opened the door and stepped into the alley.

It was empty.

The early May air had turned pleasantly warm, a hint of a breeze whispering of the summer to come. Paper and debris swirled around her feet, swept along by the wind. The sun had already set, but the full darkness of night hadn't yet arrived. In the past hour the sky had turned an ominous gray. Clouds scudded across the sky, casting a grim pallor over everything. Rain was on its way.

In spite of the warmth of the day, Katie found herself shivering.

Except for a few abandoned cars scattered about at each end of the alley, it appeared empty. Nervous and unsettled, Katie glanced around, straining to see, wondering what had happened to the man she had seen just a moment ago.

But there was no one in the alley, and especially not a man with a gun. Sighing in relief, Katie turned to go back inside when a hand landed heavily on her shoulder, causing her to let loose a screech.

Instinct had her whirling, her heart pounding in unadulterated fear. Hands clenched, her closed fist connected with something solid and hard, just as Danny, Michael and Patrick had taught her. Growing up with three boys—all hellions, to be sure—had taught her a thing or two about defending herself.

"Damn." The breath whooshed out of the stranger, and he doubled over. She was about to knee him, but something about him seemed far too familiar. Suddenly she recognized him and relief flooded through her, nearly making her faint.

"Danny?" Hesitantly she took a step closer to the doubled-over figure, laying a hand on his back. It would have been impossible to mistake that glorious head of black hair. "My God, Danny, you scared the life out of me!" Laying a hand over her pounding heart, Katie leaned back against the building and took a long, deep breath. "What on earth are you doing sneaking around the alley?"

"I'm a cop," he wheezed, holding his stomach and trying to catch his breath. "I get paid to sneak around alleys." Still holding his stomach, Danny flashed her a grin, that same incredible grin that, at sixteen, had caused her heart to pound and her knees to grow weak. It had the same effect now.

She'd always thought Danny was one of the most gorgeous men she'd ever seen. His long, lean face was just rugged enough to prevent it from being pretty.

He was nearly six feet four, with inky black hair that he wore just long enough to make him look disreputable, and his silvery blue eyes were always calm, cool and steady. Fearless. He'd always been fearless, something that had given her more than a few fits of worry. She'd always thought he looked more like a man who should be *behind* bars.

Not in front of them.

But something about him had changed in the seven years she'd been gone. Something had snuffed out the mischievous light that had always shone from his eyes, the light that had made him look as if he was running away from trouble—or square into it.

He was more solemn, serious and, at times, she thought, sad. Incredibly, achingly sad, and it hurt her heart to know something had hurt him. What, she didn't know, and couldn't ask. Seven years was a long time to be away from someone and she wasn't certain of what their relationship was anymore. Or even if they had one.

"Since when are you afraid of me, brat?" Cocking his head, he rubbed his sore belly and grunted softly. She still could pack a wallop. He'd taught her well, and the knowledge pleased him. "Besides, I thought it was Michael you were afraid of."

"When I was six, I was afraid of Michael," she reminded him with a distinctly feminine toss of her head, obviously annoyed that he still called her by her childhood nickname. It was fine when she was twelve, but he had to acknowledge that she wasn't twelve any longer—a fact he couldn't fail to notice. "And I was afraid of Michael only because he was so...serious." Planting her hands on her hips, she flashed him an arrogant look full of sass and pure female seduction. "In case you hadn't noticed, Danny, I'm no longer six." Her voice had taken on a sultry, husky quality, making his eyes widen for a fraction of a moment.

"I've noticed," he said with a bit of a frown. Since she'd come home, all he'd done was notice, and it made him darn uncomfortable.

Unable to resist, his eyes slowly slid over her. He tried not to appreciate the way her unruly red mop of hair had settled into a sleek cap of auburn curls that feathered around her beautiful face, only emphasizing those incredibly gorgeous eyes. Doe eyes, he'd always thought. The kind that held a hint of some long-ago sadness; the kind that made a man want to do something—anything—to erase that sadness.

His eyes drifted over her and he wanted to scowl. Again. That spindly, scrawny little body that had been all skinned knees and bony elbows had filled out in a way that could make a man's mouth go dry.

She wore a lemon yellow sweater cut to a vee in front that gently revealed the creamy ivory of her collarbone, and hinted at the soft womanly curves of her breasts. It wouldn't seem provocative on any other woman, but for some reason it seemed utterly provocative on her. His fingers itched to tug that vee up higher, to cover that incredibly creamy skin from anyone else's eyes.

The matching yellow skirt she wore barely grazed the tops of her knees, revealing a long, silky expanse of mouthwatering leg. The high-heeled yellow suede shoes she wore only made her legs seem to go on forever.

He had a sudden urge to drape a trench coat around her, or scold her for dressing as she had. Didn't she know it made a guy think? And want? And drool?

"I've definitely noticed," he said, his scowl deepening. He thought of giving her an affectionate, brotherly hug, as he'd once always done, but now he thought better of it. He didn't want to be reminded that little Katie wasn't so little anymore. He stuffed his hands in his pockets so he wouldn't do anything foolish.

Shifting at the look on Danny's face and in his eyes, Katie shivered and wrapped her arms around herself, secretly thrilled to know that maybe he *had* noticed she was no longer a child. It was about time. Perhaps he wasn't such a blockhead, after all.

"I didn't know it was you out here, Danny," she said carefully, warmed and yet a little unnerved by the way he was looking at her. "Julio just said there was a man with a gun at the back door. That has a tendency to put a little fear in a person." With a confident grin, she rubbed her knuckles and made another fist. "Even one who knows how to pack a punch."

He laughed and couldn't resist reaching out to capture her hand. He longed for the warm camaraderie they'd always shared. Seven years was a long time, he mused, realizing just how much he'd missed her. Running a thumb over her knuckles, he was surprised that she was as soft as a summer rain and stunned by how natural it felt to be touching her again.

"So how is the resident little tattletale?" he asked with affection.

She laughed. "He's fine. As mischievous as always."

"Guess he saw me peeking in the window." He grinned again, releasing her hand simply because the intimacy felt far too comfortable. "I wanted to make sure you were here before I came in."

In the seven months since she'd opened the center, Danny had only visited once. On Saint Patrick's Day he'd brought over the cupcakes his mother, Maeve, had made for the children. That was when he'd met Julio, who'd followed him around like a lost, lonely puppy, asking a million questions, which Danny had patiently answered. The two had become instant friends.

"Sooooo, what are you doing here, Danny?" she asked suspiciously.

"Just dropped by for a visit." Lazily leaning a shoulder against the building, he grinned at her, trying to appear casual.

"A visit?" One auburn eyebrow rose and she looked at him suspiciously. "Any particular reason why you picked *this* afternoon to pay me a visit?"

He wanted to curse. He should have known that Katie, of all people, would be able to read him like a book. She knew he never did anything without a reason.

As the late-afternoon breeze blew her hair about her face, Katie looked at him and realized that his showing up here this afternoon wasn't just a casual visit.

Distance and years had a way of changing people and relationships, but not so much that she didn't know when he was up to something. Crossing arms across her breasts, she rocked back on the heels of her shoes.

He was up to something.

Definitely.

And if she didn't know better, she would swear he was...nervous.

But that was ridiculous.

Nothing ever rattled Danny.

Danny, who'd always had a bit of the bad boy in him, was known for his confidence, his arrogance, his intense calm...and his total lack of fear.

He had a daredevil's heart and nerves of steel, combined with a bright, quick mind that allowed him to deal with any number of problems in a cool, calm manner.

When he turned his clear blue eyes on someone, they usually knew they were facing someone…dangerous. And if they had any sense, they would back off, or away.

Because Danny never would.

What she noticed most about him was his air of recklessness and confidence. He wore it like a badge. He always had, but now it was even more pronounced…and it frightened her.

Something had surely happened to him while she'd been gone. Something sad and powerful. If she hadn't known him so well, she might not have noticed.

But she did.

She knew he'd had a brief, disastrous marriage, and that it had broken up, suddenly, inexplicably, and that he had offered no explanations to anyone. Not his brothers, his mother, not even Da, his beloved grandfather. He'd discussed his failed marriage with no one.

The family, wanting to respect his privacy, had cautiously and deliberately sidestepped the issue, not prying or questioning. It didn't matter what had happened; what mattered was that the family was always there to offer comfort, support, whatever he needed, whenever he needed it.

Although Katie knew very little about his brief marriage, she didn't have to be told that somehow, some way he'd been very, very hurt. For a moment she wondered if it was what had put the bleak sadness in his eyes.

Still staring at him, knowledge came as if whispered in her ear by a great sage. "Are you in trouble?" she asked suddenly, her eyes widening in alarm.

Shaking his head, he laughed. "Now, is that nice? I stop by to pay you a friendly visit and you immediately think I'm in trouble."

"It may not be nice, Danny," she muttered dryly. "But it's probably the truth." She studied him, a frown creasing her brow. "All right, Danny. 'Fess up. What's going on?"

"I brought you something." Glancing down the alley to

where he parked the car, he narrowed his gaze, hoping his precious package was still doing all right.

She'd fallen asleep on the way over here. Either that, or his constant attempt at baby chatter had lulled her right over the edge into boredom.

Suddenly pleased, Katie couldn't help the smile that tilted her lips. "You brought me a present?"

He laughed. "Just like a woman to assume it's a present."

Crossing her arms across her breasts, she scowled at him. "Unless it's the mumps, Danny, when a man announces he's brought me something, I'm going to assume it's a present."

Shaking his head, he laughed again. He'd forgotten about that viperous tongue of hers, which could best him and everyone else every time. He and his brothers might have had brute strength, but Katie had the quick mental ability and the fast mouth.

"A present is probably a correct assumption in most cases," he admitted with a slow nod of his head.

"But not this one?" she asked suspiciously.

"Not…exactly." He glanced down the alley again. "Wait here, Katie." He turned and slowly headed down the alley, while she waited, rubbing her hands up and down her arms in nervousness.

Her eyes widened when he went to one of the cars parked at the end of the alley, opened the back door, then slowly lifted something out. She couldn't tell what it was because it was wrapped in a blanket.

She didn't wait for him to get to her, but started walking toward him. Something about the look on his face made the hair on the back of her neck stand on end. When she reached him, their eyes met and held.

"I need a favor, Katie," he said quietly, his gaze steady on hers. It made her pulse dance. They'd always had the ability to communicate without words, something that used to drive his brothers crazy. They could simply look at each other and know what the other was thinking. She was grateful to learn some things hadn't changed.

Katie shifted her gaze to the bundle in his arms. "Does this…favor have anything to do with what's in that blanket?" she asked quietly, fearing the answer.

Danny let out a long sigh. "Yeah." He glanced down at the blanket for a moment and his gaze softened. "I need you to help me take care of something." At her look of suspicion, he quickly added, "Just for a little while."

"And is this 'something' under that blanket?" she asked cautiously, a multitude of thoughts racing through her mind.

Before he could answer, the blanket stirred, and a small, red head popped out. Wide blue eyes blinked as the baby swiveled her head, taking in her surroundings. Seemingly satisfied, she nestled her head on Danny's chest. One small, chubby fist clutched his shirt, while the other went in her mouth as she promptly snuggled back in and went right to sleep.

Katie's startled gaze went from the baby to Danny. "Uh, Danny, do you, uh, want to tell me what's going on?" Unable to resist, she ran a gentle hand over the back of the baby's head. It was damp from sweat and sleep.

"If I knew, I'd be happy to tell you, Katie." Lifting his gaze, Danny shrugged.

"If you knew?" she asked with the lift of her eyebrow. Katie shook her head, trying to understand. "All right. Let's take this from the top. Who is she? And why do you need me to help you take care of her?" The first seeds of fear began nibbling at her nerve endings. "Where are her parents?"

Danny blew out a breath. "I don't know anything about her. Katie, I need your help."

"Danny, wait a minute here." Deliberately she lowered her voice so as not to alarm the baby. She was alarmed enough for both of them. "You don't know what's going on? You don't know who she is, and you don't know who her parents are?"

He grinned, making her fear grow. "That about covers it."

"Oh my word." Annoyed at his deliberate brevity, Katie shook her head. "All right. Let's start with some basics, then. Exactly *where* did you get her? She certainly didn't drop from the heavens, did she?" she asked suspiciously, knowing, with Danny, you could never be sure of anything.

"Just about." He shifted the baby to his other arm, carefully tucking the blanket up around her neck to ward off the wind that had kicked up. The sky was getting increasingly dark with the promise of rain. "I found her sitting in the front seat of my Mustang when I got off duty tonight."

Katie's eyes widened in shock. "You *found* her? You mean someone just…just…*left* her in your car? Abandoned her?" Her voice wavered. The mistreatment of children—especially helpless babies—never failed to arouse her anger.

"Yep."

"Oh, God, the poor little tyke." Her heart immediately softened toward the child. The thought that someone could willingly abandon their own baby—their own flesh and blood—brought out her anger, as well as all her protective instincts. Gently, she rubbed the baby's back and the little tyke squirmed, snuggling closer to Danny. "But why?" She nearly shivered in revulsion. "Why on earth would anyone abandon their baby?"

It was a rhetorical question. There were myriad reasons, not any of them logical—at least to her—but obviously they were to someone.

"I've been asking myself that same question for the past hour." He shook his head, trying to bank down the anger he felt at the nameless person who'd so heartlessly abandoned their own child.

"I checked everything. There were no identifying marks, no name, no note, nothing to explain what the heck is going on.'' His gaze met and held Katie's. "I don't have a clue who she is. Or why they left her in my car.'' Absently he stroked the baby's back in a soothing gesture. His gaze and his voice softened. "But she's a cutie, isn't she?''

Katie couldn't help but smile. Danny always tried so hard not to show people his soft side, but *she'd* always known when something mattered to him. And she had a feeling this baby—whoever she was—mattered a great deal to him.

"She's adorable,'' Katie admitted as her gaze slowly shifted from the baby to him. "Danny,'' she said, choosing her words carefully. "You realize if she's been abandoned, you have to report it to DCFS.''

There was a long, silent pause. Danny's jaw tightened stubbornly. She knew that look and knew it well. "Oh, no,'' she muttered with a shake of her head, knowing what was coming. "Danny, you can't possibly think...you can't even consider...'' She broke off, running a nervous hand through her hair. "You're not turning her over to DCFS, are you?''

"Not on a bad bet,'' he said with a determined shake of his head. "I'm not about to throw this kid into the system. What she needs now is some special attention and tender loving care, things she'd never get if I turned her over to the state. She'd just get lost in the system.'' He glanced down at the baby, then kissed the top of her sleeping head. "I'm not going to let that happen,'' he said quietly. "Not to her. I can't.''

Uh-oh.

Katie was beginning to get that shaky, nervous feeling in her stomach. The same feeing she'd always gotten when they were little and Danny or one of his brothers tried to drag her into whatever mischief they'd gotten themselves into.

Fear raced over her and she inhaled a slow, deep breath, wiping her suddenly sweaty palms on her skirt. "Danny, be reasonable. You know the rules better than anyone. You know—''

"No, Katie." He shook his head. ''I'm not going to do it.'' He snared a free arm around her shoulder and drew her close. "Here's what I figured…'' He tilted his head close so he could whisper in her ear, wondering as he did about the intoxicating scent she wore and why he'd never noticed it before. "Obviously whoever left this kid in my car did it for a reason, right?'' He didn't give her a chance to answer. "I figure maybe they just needed a break. You know the neighborhood, Katie. It shouldn't be too hard to figure out who dumped their kid. Hell, everyone knows everyone else's business. Someone's gotta know something about this kid. It shouldn't take us too long to figure out who she belongs to.''

"Us?'' She narrowed her gaze. "What's with this 'us,' Danny?''

Her heart began to pound. She wasn't sure if it was because of his nearness. Or her own fear. He still had an arm draped around her shoulder. His warm breath fanned her face, and he was so close she could smell the familiar masculine scent of him. A scent that had always represented safety, security, home, Danny. It was hard to think when he was so close. She tried to pull back, but he held on.

"Danny.'' She swallowed, trying to hide her sudden nervousness at his closeness. "While you're out looking for the parents or responsible party, who's going to be looking out for the baby?''

He kept looking at her until realization dawned. Immediately she shook her head as fear skittered over her.

"Oh, no.'' She shook her head harder and raised both hands in the air as if to ward off evil. "Absolutely not.''

He just grinned at her, the same grin that had been her undoing for most of her life. She muttered a pithy oath under her breath.

He was *not* going to do this to her, she thought, strengthening her resolve. She was not about to let him drag her into this. She couldn't. She had too many other people depending on her. She couldn't make a decision of this magnitude without taking into consideration all that was at risk. It wasn't just herself and the center, but all the other children, as well.

"Are you out of your mind?" she demanded, her voice rising despite her attempt to curb the panic that had hit her the moment he returned with a wayward baby in tow. "Reckless and dangerous are one thing, Danny. Stupidity is quite another."

"Now, Kat, it's not that bad. It's not like I…kidnapped her or anything."

She took a deep breath, trying to decide if she should hit him. Or reason with him.

Reasoning was out. But not by much.

"Danny, come on, you know the rules as well as I do. Any violations could result in you losing your badge and me losing my license. This is serious. A helpless human being is at stake here." She could see her words were falling on deaf ears. "Who knows, Danny? With something like this, we might even end up behind bars." The mere thought made her shudder. "And may I remind you I don't look good in prison stripes?"

He just looked at her, a sad, hopeful expression on his face.

"We cannot do this, Danny," she said firmly, shaking her head. "We simply can't."

He *was* trying to drag her into his craziness, just as he had done when they were children. Then, she'd foolishly gone along with all his wild schemes—never mind that, more times than not, they'd both gotten caught and ended up in big trouble.

Well, they weren't children anymore, and she wasn't about to let him drag her into this. She was a businesswoman, and in order to keep her business there were certain rules and regulations she had to follow. If she didn't, she could lose everything she'd worked toward her whole life.

"Katie." The soft seductive tone of his voice sent a trembling shiver over her. He lifted a hand and laid it gently on her cheek as his gaze met hers. "Listen," he said softly, stroking her cheek. "We can't simply abandon her, can we?" His sweet, sad gaze searched hers, and she felt herself weakening. "She doesn't have anyone, hon." He glanced down at the baby, then back up at her. "She's all alone in the world. Seems to me that you, more than anyone else, should be able to understand how important it is for us to take care of her."

Katie was so close, the hint of her perfume was tickling his senses. He never realized how intoxicating it was. It was familiar, yet held a sensual lure that made him think of things he had no business thinking. Especially about Katie.

Struggling to keep his mind on the conversation and not on the images that had suddenly, inexplicably popped into his head, Danny looked at her carefully. "It's not like you to turn your back on someone who's helpless and all alone in the world. Especially a child."

The aching sadness in his voice caused tears to form before she could stop them. They filled her eyes and forced her to swallow back the sudden constriction in her throat.

All alone in the world.

She remembered all too well what it felt like to be abandoned, to be left all alone in the world with no one who cared about her.

It was something that remained with her every day.

Her gaze shifted to the baby sleeping soundly, *safely* in Danny's arms. She felt her heart constrict when she thought of how helpless the child was, how totally, unbearably alone.

She'd been the same way at one time. What would have happened to her if Aunt Maeve and Uncle Jock hadn't been there to take her in, to take care of her?

If Danny, Michael, Patrick and Da hadn't been there for her?

She couldn't even begin to imagine.

They had taken her into their hearts and their home and loved her, making her feel like one of their own.

Her gaze shifted to Danny and her resolve faltered. It was Danny who had rescued her from a world that had suddenly seemed strange, huge and incredibly frightening.

Danny whom she'd clung to when she was scared at night, or when the recurring nightmares plagued her. Danny who sat and held her hand and told her silly stories or jokes, or played board games or read to her until her tears dried and her nightmares faded.

Danny who sat with her every time his mother and father went out because she feared, like her own parents, they would never return.

Danny who would coax her into eating—practically spoon-feeding her—when her stomach acted up and she couldn't even bear the thought—let alone the smell—of food.

It was Danny who had walked her to and from school each and every day because everything was so new, so foreign and so terribly frightening.

Danny who had bloodied his knuckles and another little boy's nose for calling her a carrot head when she was barely eight years old.

Danny had always been there for her. No matter what.

And now he wanted to be there for another little girl who had been left all alone in the world with no one to care for her.

How could she refuse to help him?

Katie dashed at her eyes. She'd never deliberately turned her back on a child who needed her. Not ever. It just wasn't in her nature.

Because of her own past, she'd worked her whole life to be able to help children who were too young or too helpless to help themselves. So how could she turn her back on a man who'd done so much for her, and a baby who so obviously needed her?

She couldn't, she realized dully. No matter what the consequences. No matter what the price. No matter what the rules and regulations.

Rules and regulations were fine, and certainly had their place, but they didn't take into account what was in a person's heart.

There was no way she could knowingly or willingly turn her back on Danny or the unknown baby.

"Blast it, Danny." Sniffling, she swiped at her eyes. "That's emotional blackmail and you know it."

"Details, details, Kat." Grinning, he dug in his pocket and handed her a freshly pressed handkerchief. "So what do you say? Will you help me?" he asked, dropping an arm around her shoulder again and snagging her close in a familiar gesture he'd done a million times in the past, except this time it seemed totally, utterly different.

He'd never been so aware of Katie as a…woman before. It shook him, leaving him off balance for a moment, and women *never* shook his balance. What the heck was going on?

"It's only for a little while—a couple of hours at best. What harm will it do? And besides, who'll even know? I promise I'll never tell. Come on, Kat." Tilting her chin up, he forced her to look at him. Their gazes met, clung. He couldn't help but notice how soft and curved her unpainted mouth was. How full and bow shaped her lips. Suddenly he wondered how she would taste. The thought nearly frightened him out of his shoes, and he shifted his gaze and his thoughts, thoroughly annoyed with himself.

"This is dirty pool, Daniel Sullivan," she accused, glaring at him for a moment, knowing in her heart the battle was already lost. Exasperated, she blew out a long, slow breath. "All right, all right." She raised her hands in surrender and rolled her eyes toward the heavens. "So I'll get used to wearing stripes. And when they strip me of my license and shut down my day-care center, I can get a job handing out cigarettes to inmates. Maybe," she added with a resigned sigh.

"I knew I could count on you, Katie." Gently, he stroked a finger down her cheek, not understanding why he needed to touch her again. Probably just gratitude and relief.

"Have you ever doubted it?" she asked dryly.

"Maybe a time or two. Thanks, Kat." He flashed the famous Sullivan grin, wondering again about the scent she was wearing. It was something spicy and very sensual that made him think of hot nights and steamy sex. Didn't she know better than to wear that kind of perfume? It could give a guy ideas.

"Let's go," he said, abruptly grabbing her elbow and ushering her along with him as he started back down the alley in the opposite direction of his car.

Startled, she let him guide her along. For a moment. "Go?" Shaking her head in confusion, she skidded to a halt. "Go?" she repeated, stunned. She dug in her heels, glancing back at the center for a moment. "Daniel Patrick Sullivan, where on earth do you think I'm going?" She didn't give him a chance to answer. The baby murmured, then shifted, so Katie gave her a reassuring pat on the back, before standing on tiptoe to glower at Danny.

"Would you mind telling me exactly what it is we're doing? I can't just up and leave the center without telling Mrs. Hennypenny where I'm going. I have responsibilities. Children who are depending on me." Her temper simmering at his high-handedness, she shook her elbow free of him. "And stop dragging me along like a puppy."

"A puppy?" he repeated with a grin and a lift of his brow, making her want to smack him. The wind was picking up, blowing his dark hair around his face. "Now, Kat, would I treat you like that?"

"You have and you did. Now I'm not moving another inch until you tell me where we're going."

He sighed, glancing at the baby. "I thought I just explained all that to you," he said with deliberate patience, ignoring her scowl. "To find the kid's parents. Now, where's your car parked?" he asked, taking her elbow and abruptly turning them around and starting down the alley in the opposite direction.

She blinked. "*My* car?" She came to another halt and Danny sighed heavily. "What on earth do you need my car for?" she asked suspiciously.

"We can't all fit in my car," he said patiently. "It's a two seater, remember? We've got the kid, the kid contraption, you and me. We need your station wagon."

"It's parked in the lot at the end of the alley." She pointed in the same direction he'd turned them in, wondering why she'd just told him where her car was. But Danny had always had the ability to coax her into doing things she knew better than to do. "I'm not going anywhere until I check in with Mrs. Hennypenny. I can't just up and take off, Danny. I have responsibilities, remember?" With him around she was lucky she could remember her name, never mind anything else. She began to wonder if she was going to regret her decision. She glanced at the sleeping baby in his arms and realized, no matter what happened, she couldn't regret her decision. This baby needed her. And so did Danny. She would help him.

If she didn't strangle him first.

"Details, details," he muttered again, reluctantly following her toward the center's back door. "But could you make it quick, Kat? Let's not advertise to the whole world that we've got the kid. That's why I want you and the kid with me, rather than here at the center. The less people who know about this, the better."

"You mean the less people who know, the less chance we have of getting caught?" He grinned and she wanted to smack him again. She understood his logic now, but it might have been helpful had he explained his intentions *before* he started dragging her around.

Danny glanced up and down the alley, then at the sky.

"Besides, it's getting dark and it looks like it's gonna rain. I want to cruise the neighborhood, see what I can find out, before everyone bolts indoors. Someone's got to know something." Gently, he rubbed the baby's back in a soothing motion, crooning softly to her.

Exhaling a deep breath, Katie nodded. "So what do you propose I tell Mrs. Hennypenny?"

He looked thoughtful for a moment, then he grinned that heart-stopping grin. "Tell her you've got an emergency and you have to leave." She opened her mouth to protest, but he gave a friendly push to get her moving. "Go, Kat. Daylight's burning."

Burning.

She hoped like heck that when this was all over, daylight was the only thing burning. She glanced at the baby in Danny's arms again and sighed in resignation.

Because she definitely, positively did not look good in prison stripes!

Chapter Three

"**Y**ou're worrying again, Kat," Danny said, glancing across the seat at her as he expertly maneuvered her station wagon around a turn. For the past hour they'd been driving up and down the familiar neighborhood streets. Several times Danny had stopped abruptly, pulled over to a corner, then jumped out to question someone while she stayed in the car tending to the baby, who had blissfully fallen asleep after drinking a bottle.

So far they'd learned nothing. No one in the neighborhood knew anything about the baby, or who might have abandoned her.

"I told you to stop worrying. Everything's gonna be fine." He flashed her a grin. "Would this face lie?"

"Don't tempt me to answer that," she retorted, as he reached across the baby seat and tugged down the hem of her skirt so that it covered more of her leg. "Stop that," she said, slapping his hand away. "That's the second time you've pulled on my hem. Why do you keep doing that?" she asked in annoyance.

"Your skirt's too short," he announced, still scanning the sidewalk and not bothering to look at her.

"My skirt's too—" Her voice broke off as her eyes darkened and her nostrils flared. He was doing his "big brother" act again. The temptation to smack him was getting stronger by the minute. "Excuse me, Danny, but since when did you become a fashion expert?"

"I don't need to be an expert to know when a woman's showing too much leg." He was still studying the street. A group of teens were huddled in front of the Logan Square Youth Center. He was debating whether to pull over and question them or not. "It can give a guy ideas."

She wanted to smack him again. It certainly hadn't given him any ideas!

Smiling smugly, she toed off her heels and crossed her legs, allowing more leg to show in a deliberate display of defiance. "For your information, Danny, Sam happens to like my short skirts. And my legs," she added softly, deliberately smoothing her wool skirt over her thighs.

He glanced at the long expanse of leg that was showing, and nearly swerved into the other lane.

"And Sam doesn't need me to give him any ideas." She laughed suddenly. The sound was delicate, feathering up his spine. "Trust me, he has plenty of his own."

Danny's head swiveled around, the teen boys huddled in the corner forgotten for a moment. He narrowed his gaze on her in the darkened car, trying to keep his gaze and his mind off her legs. "Who the blazes is Sam, and what business is it of his how short your skirts are?" His voice had dropped to a deadly decibel. "And what the hell kind of ideas are we talking about here?"

"Stop looking at me, and look at the road," she cried, grabbing the wheel. She wanted him to notice her, but she didn't want to get them killed in the process.

"Spill it, Kat." He glared out the windshield. "Who is this Sam guy?" He did not like the sound of things. And he was absolutely certain he didn't like this Sam, whoever he was. He knew what kind of ideas a guy entertained when faced with a short skirt and long, gorgeous legs. For a moment he wished Katie's legs were still bony, bruised and spindly. At least then he wouldn't have to worry about some guy ogling her.

Katie smiled, enjoying the look on his face, not certain if it was concern or jealousy, but pleased nonetheless. "Not every man sees me as a kid, Danny." She ran a hand slowly through her hair, then licked her lips in an action deliberately meant to be provocative.

Danny tightened his hand on the wheel as his eyes followed the movement of her tongue. His mouth went dry as dust. He wondered again what she would taste like. More importantly, he wondered exactly who else had been tasting her. Kissing her. This mysterious Sam? he wondered. The thought made his fists tighten on the wheel.

"And what exactly does Sam see you as?" he demanded, not certain he wanted to know. He felt a flash of something constrict in his gut. It wasn't jealousy, he told himself. It couldn't be. He'd never been jealous a day in his life. It wasn't in his nature.

There were plenty of women to go around. Plenty. And he'd always had his fair share. He planned on keeping it that way.

Never again would he be snared by just one. Snared, betrayed and heartbroken. No, he'd gone the one-man-one-woman route. Had pledged a lifetime of love, honesty, trust. Marriage. Commitment. Family. The whole nine yards. He'd bought it, believed it, as all the Sullivans did. It was how they'd been raised. To believe in the sanctity of marriage and the happily ever after until death do you part. As his parents and grandparents had done before him.

Unfortunately, he never got quite that far. His marriage had disintegrated within six months amid a barrage of deceit and lies, and he'd vowed then never to allow himself to be vulnerable to one woman again.

It was too big of a risk—too painful—to put your hopes,

your trust and your love in one person's hands. He'd learned that bitter lesson a bit too late. He would never go through that emotional wringer again.

He was the only Sullivan ever to break his vows and end his marriage. It wasn't a distinction he was proud of, which was probably why he'd never spoken about his brief, very disastrous marriage with anyone. Why let the whole world know he'd been fooled? Duped? Especially his family. It was bad enough *he* knew. It was a pain he would have to live with the rest of his life.

"Sam sees me as a woman, Danny," Katie announced simply, pretending to be immensely interested in tucking the blanket higher around the sleeping baby. The little tyke looked so fragile, so peaceful and content snuggled into the one-piece sleeper Danny had insisted on buying her, along with several other changes of clothes, formula, bottles and, of course, the necessities of baby life: disposable diapers and a pacifier.

"Sam sees you as a woman, huh?" he muttered, as if the very idea was foreign to him. "Who the hell is this Sam, anyway?" he asked with a scowl. He wasn't anyone from the neighborhood, at least not anyone Danny knew, and he thought he knew everyone.

"Just a...friend," she said, deliberately being evasive. In actuality, Sam was a sixty-two-year-old widower who worked part-time at the pharmacy two doors down from the center. He and Mrs. Hennypenny had been an item for the past six months. They both enjoyed bridge and played regularly with Sam's widowed brother, who was almost seventy and as crotchety and cantankerous as a wet cat. Occasionally they invited her to join them when they needed a fourth for bridge, and she'd accepted simply for lack of anything better to do.

No, Sam didn't think of her as a kid or a sister. More like a granddaughter, she thought in amusement, but she wasn't about to tell Danny that.

"Friend, huh?" he muttered darkly, abruptly swerving

across the street and braking at the curb. He leaned across her to open the window. His arm brushed against her breasts and she inhaled sharply as her body tingled in alarm. "Martha," he called, then glanced at the baby, fearful of waking her up. "Come on over here. I need to talk to you."

Katie watched as an old woman stepped out of a darkened doorway and shuffled toward his car. She was wearing a ragged black raincoat two sizes too big for her. It dragged on the ground as she walked. On her feet she wore a pair of snazzy red shoes with black argyle socks rolled down to her ankles. She was clutching a large paper shopping bag that looked as if it was stuffed with all her worldly possessions.

"Hey, Danny," she said as she shuffled toward the car. She gave Katie a cursory glance and a smile. "How you doing? How'd you like my new shoes?" Martha clicked her heels together like a latter-day Dorothy from the Wizard of Oz, obviously delighted by her new foot gear. "Told you I'd buy shoes with the money." She nodded her head. "Yessiree, I'd never break a promise to you, Danny. I put the money you gave me to real good use." She clicked her heels again. "So what do you think?"

Craning his neck to see, Danny nodded his head in approval as he appraised her latest footwear. "They're great, Martha. Real lookers." He cocked his head and studied the woman, apparently unfazed by her bedraggled appearance. "I want you to meet someone, Martha." He shifted, dropping his hand to Katie's shoulder and tugging up the vee of her sweater in the process. "This here's Katie."

Martha grinned, revealing a row of missing teeth. "Your kid sister, the one you always been talking about?" Delighted, she reached in the car and grabbed Katie's hand and began pumping it. "My, my, look at you. You're a beauty, aren't you?"

Warmed by the woman's kindness, Katie smiled. "Thank you. It's very nice to meet you, Martha." She glanced at Danny. She would deal with this "kid sister" nonsense later.

The old woman threw her head back and hooted. "Me?" She laughed some more. "Sure ain't a pleasure to meet me, honey, but it's real polite to hear you say so." Self-consciously, she pressed one hand down the front of her tattered coat and held on to Katie with the other. "So whaddya up to, Danny?"

"Not too much," he said evasively. If Martha noticed the bundle of joy in the front seat, she'd wisely chosen to ignore it. "Tell me, how's that granddaughter of yours doing? Is she feeling better now?"

Martha grinned, pride glinting in her eyes. "She's doing real well now, Danny. Thanks for asking."

"Martha's granddaughter is a senior at the University of Illinois," he explained.

"An honor student. Studying medicine," Martha injected proudly. "Got a full scholarship she did. Gonna be a doctor." Martha grinned, rocking back on her dazzling red shoes. "Imagine, my granddaughter a doctor. Her mama, she woulda been real proud." Her eyes misted for a moment. "Real proud."

"Martha, did you eat today?" Danny glanced out the windshield with a frown. Thick fat drops of rain had begun to fall. He turned back to the old woman.

"Naw, not yet." She glanced down the street. "I'll get something at the shelter later."

"Come on," he said, reaching in the back seat and unlocking the door. He knew the shelter had stopped serving dinner hours ago. "We'll give you a lift to the shelter. But first we'll pick up something to eat on the way. Katie and I haven't had dinner, either." He cast a sideward glance at Katie, who looked as though she wanted to hug him in spite of her aggravation with him.

This was the Danny she had fallen in love with, Katie thought. A man who protected helpless children and fed harmless old ladies while still allowing them their dignity.

"What's that you got in the front seat, Danny?" Martha asked as she settled herself and her shopping bag in the back seat with a sigh. "Looks like a baby."

Danny laughed. "It is a baby," he said, pulling away from the curb.

"What's her name?"

Bewildered, Katie and Danny looked at each other. "Her, uh, name?" Danny repeated, looking at Katie for help.

"Molly," Katie said abruptly, earning a smile from Danny. "Her name is Molly." Or at least it would be for the time being.

"Molly," Martha repeated with a nod, as if considering. "Nice name. Is she yours?" She leaned forward to stare at Katie and the baby with interest.

"Nope," Danny said before Katie had a chance to. "The kid's not Katie's. In fact, I was hoping maybe you might recognize her."

Martha spent all of her time outdoors, except for the cool nights when he tried to find her an empty bed in a shelter. If the shelter was full, he knew she slept outside. He'd warned her over and over again that it was too dangerous for her to be sleeping outside, but she wouldn't listen.

Martha stared at the baby for a long moment, then slowly shook her head. "Nope. Don't believe I've ever seen her before." She leaned back against the seat, making herself comfortable. "She's cute though, isn't she?"

"Definitely," Danny said with a laugh, glancing at the baby as he pulled through a fast-food drive-in. "Angelo's all right with you?" He was talking to Martha, but looking at Katie, and her heart tumbled over. Angelo's was a shared memory from the past—something from their childhood— and it touched her that he'd remembered. She thought of saying something, then thought better of it, not wanting to embarrass him in front of his friend.

"What would you like, Martha?" he asked.

Squinting, she leaned forward and read the menu with

interest. "Could I maybe have one of those double hamburgers with lots of ketchup. And some French fries?" She tapped Danny's shoulder. "And tell them onions. Lots of onions. And a big orange soda pop." She laughed as Danny placed their order, tapping Katie on the shoulder. "I love orange soda pop."

Katie laughed. "So do I."

Danny cast a sideward glance at Katie, relieved that she hadn't been put off by Martha. But he needn't have worried. This was Katie. Not one of those slick, saucy, seductive women he was used to dating, who flitted in and out of his life with no more impact than a butterfly. The kind of woman he usually dated would have wrinkled her nose at sharing their time, let alone a car, with someone like Martha.

Once they had their order, Danny pulled back onto the street and headed toward the shelter. Because the weather had finally warmed up, he hoped they would still have some empty beds.

"I'll be right back," he said as he swerved to the curb and threw the car in park. "Will you two be all right?" he asked worriedly, glancing first at the sleeping baby, then at Katie.

She smiled. "Fine, Danny. Go get Martha settled."

He gave the baby another swift glance, then slid out of the car. He helped Martha to the building, holding her arm, her food and her shopping bag. It was still raining and he hustled her along, trying to keep her dry.

Martha loped over puddles, trying not to get her snazzy red shoes wet, and the sight made Katie smile.

Shoes. Danny had bought the woman shoes. Shaking her head, Katie stifled a yawn, wondering why it should surprise her. Danny's heart was like a marshmallow, especially for someone—anyone—in need. Which was one of the reasons she'd fallen in love with him so many years ago.

But that was then, and this was now, she scolded herself. She couldn't—wouldn't—allow herself to be hurt again. Or rejected. She wasn't about to let her feelings or her imagination run haywire. She wasn't fourteen anymore, but a grown woman. And in spite of the fact that she and Danny had been thrown together by circumstances beyond their control, she wasn't about to start spinning dreams about happily ever after.

She would help Danny as she'd promised, but that was it. She would keep her feelings and her dreams to herself. Danny couldn't seem to accept her as a woman, and she couldn't accept anything less.

Yawning again with fatigue, Katie checked the baby, then glanced at the building that Danny and Martha had disappeared into. A run-down three-story brick that took up half a city block, it had once been a school that had been closed, abandoned and then turned into a shelter for the homeless.

The scent of the food suddenly reminded her that she hadn't eaten lunch or dinner, and she was starving. It must have had an effect on the baby as well, because she began squirming and fussing. Katie unhooked the seat belt and picked her up, crooning and rocking her until she quieted.

Holding her close, Katie's eyes slid closed. Holding this little tyke brought out all her maternal instincts. She'd always wanted a home, a husband, her own family. As much as she'd wanted the center, she truly believed she could have it all. A career and a family. Of course, growing up, she'd always thought that family would be with Danny. She swallowed the lump that had suddenly formed in her throat. Being so close to him again made it hard to control her feelings—and her disappointment.

It was hard to let go of her dream, especially when Danny was the only man she'd ever wanted.

But she would do it if she had to. She had no other choice.

Swallowing hard, she concentrated on the baby in her arms. She nuzzled Molly, savoring the sweet, baby scent of her. The child's cheeks were chubby and rosy, and her

little lips were pursed in displeasure. Katie ran her hand
down the baby's backside, grinning when she realized what
the problem was.

Obviously what they needed here was a change—of diaper and scenery. The baby couldn't sleep in a car seat all
night. She needed to be changed, fed again and put down
for the night. The question of where Molly was going to
spend the night was still up in the air, only increasing Katie's worry.

Still crooning softly to the baby, she watched as the sky
opened up and a torrential downpour began. Through the
darkened gangway between the shelter and its neighboring
building, she saw Danny sprint toward the car. By the time
he yanked open the door, his clothes were plastered against
his skin.

"You're going to catch pneumonia," she scolded as he
slicked wet hair back from his forehead. "Did you get Martha settled?" She handed him one of the extra receiving
blankets they had bought so he could wipe his face and
hair off.

He sneezed, then nodded, rubbing the blanket over his
wet hair. "Yep. At least for tonight I know she'll be safe
and dry."

"Shoes?" Katie said with a grin, taking the blanket from
him. "You bought her a pair of shoes?"

"No, *she* bought them," he clarified with a smile,
slightly embarrassed.

"Ahh, but you gave her the money, right?" Teasing mischief shone in her eyes.

He waved a hand in the air as if dismissing his contri-
bution. "Details, Kat. Minor details."

Details? She wanted to hug him. Only Danny would
think buying a street person a pair of shoes was a minor
detail.

"How's she doing?" he asked, glancing at the baby and
seemingly oblivious to his near drowned state.

"She's wet, and I think she's hungry again." Her gaze

met his. "Danny, she can't sleep in this car seat all night. It's too uncomfortable."

He sighed, glancing out at the darkened, now-empty street. It was pouring so hard he could barely see out the windshield. "I know," he said softly, thinking. Impatient, he drummed his fingers on the steering wheel. "Katie, it's been almost three hours since I found her. It's dark and raining now. The streets are empty and probably will be as long as this rain keeps up. There's not much chance of us learning anything else tonight."

"I know." Katie held the baby closer as a shaft of light lit the sky. "So what are we going to do with her?" she asked softly. Her questioning gaze met his. "Are we going to turn her over to DCFS now?" Emotions tugged at her heart. In just three short hours she'd gotten incredibly attached to this little tyke. Molly was so helpless, so small and so unbearably alone, Katie couldn't help letting her heart get ensnared.

Danny looked at Katie for a long, silent moment. A splash of light from a street lamp glowed on her skin, and for an instant he was distracted by the softness of her skin, her features, that incredibly unbelievable mouth. He reached out and touched Katie's hair. It was like silk, making his fingers itch to touch more. Quickly, he banished the thought, wondering again where it had come from.

"Molly?" he said with a lift of his brow and a smile, still caressing a strand of her hair and trying to divert her attention from the problem at hand. "How'd you come up with the name Molly?" It was his late grandmother's name, a grandmother he'd never met, but had grown to know and love through his grandfather Da's infamous stories.

Katie grinned. "I grew up in the same house as you. I listened to Da's stories, as well." She shrugged, realizing he was pleased. "It was the first name that came to mind."

"I'm glad," he said softly, looking at her and wondering what the heck was happening. This was Katie, who was as familiar to him as his own name. He knew her as well as he knew himself, and with that knowledge came a certain calm and peace, and a certain level of comfortable ease.

And yet, there was something entirely different about her now, or perhaps it was simply the way he was responding to her, which confounded him. And women *never* confounded him.

Especially one he knew so well.

Yet, there was something about her—maybe it was something about *him*; he wasn't really sure anymore—that made him feel as if he didn't really know Katie, and it both confused and beguiled him.

In actuality it was driving him nuts.

"Danny?" He was staring at her with a look that was making her nervous. And incredibly aware of him. "Are we going to turn Molly over to DCFS now?" There really was no other logical choice, she thought. Surely he would have to see that now. But the thought brought a sharp shaft of pain to her heart.

"I can't, Katie," he whispered. His finger slid to her chin and he tilted her face toward him. Their eyes met and held in the darkness, and Katie swallowed hard. She could see that haunting sadness in his eyes, that bleak hopelessness that made her heart ache.

Whatever had put that sadness in Danny's eyes, she somehow had a feeling it was connected to this baby. How, she wasn't certain.

Why else would he be so adamant about not turning Molly over to DCFS? Intrigued and a bit perplexed, Katie wished she could ask Danny about it. Ask what had happened to take the mischievous sparkle out of his eyes, replacing it with such heavy sadness, but she couldn't. She wouldn't pry. It wasn't her style. Danny had to tell her himself—if and when he wanted to.

"I just need a little more time, Kat." His thumb caressed her chin, softly, gently, lulling her with a seductive promise. "We didn't have much of a chance to learn anything."

"Danny, we don't know any more about her now than

we did three hours ago," she said, her voice whisper soft. He was silent for a moment, the only noise the soft, repetitive rhythm of the windshield wipers. Rain tapped softly on the roof of the car, creating a staccato beat as the dark of night wrapped around them in an intimate embrace.

"True," he finally admitted. "But tomorrow, in the light of day, I'm sure we'll be able to find out who she belongs to and return her." He brushed a hand across the top of the now-sleeping baby's head. Her hair was as soft and silky as Katie's, and almost the same color. He wondered why he hadn't realized it before. His gaze shifted from the baby to Katie. They could be mother and daughter, their coloring was so similar. For some reason the thought caused an ache in his gut—in his heart.

"And if we don't, Danny?" she asked quietly. Her words seemed to reverberate in the quiet car. "What if we don't find out anything about her tomorrow?" She was still holding the baby, cuddling her close, her arms already aching at the thought of having them empty once again. But she realized they had to do what was right for the baby.

"We will," he promised, as if merely saying the words would will it. His gaze met Katie's again. She could see the sadness in them—the hope—and she could no more turn away from him than she could sprout wings and fly.

"All right," she said with a resigned sigh. "Just for tonight." She pressed a gentle kiss to the baby's hair. She could handle this for one more night without having a heart attack. She hoped. "But if we don't learn anything, then we turn her over to DCFS. Agreed?"

He didn't answer, merely grinned that heart-stopping grin. "Thanks, Kat. I knew I could count on you." Leaning close, he went to kiss her cheek just as she turned her head to say something to him. His mouth touched the corner of her mouth—the soft, unpainted mouth that had been tormenting him all evening. He felt as if a bolt of lightning had shot through his system, nearly sizzling his nerves. Instinctively, his body reacted with pure male awareness.

Stunned, he jerked back, eyes wide, senses reeling, wondering what the blazes had happened. He stared at her, tempted to touch his mouth, but he didn't need to do that to know it was still tingling.

What was going on? he wondered in confusion. He hadn't reacted to a woman's kiss like that—and it wasn't even that much of a kiss, he reminded himself—since he was fourteen and had stolen his very first kiss from Mary Lou Keating at the school picnic. She'd belted him one, right in the chops, but it was nothing compared to the punch he'd felt when his lips had touched pure female for the first time.

He'd never felt that way again.

Until just now.

With Katie.

He sure as hell wasn't fourteen anymore.

And he'd done a lot more kissing since then.

But he'd never felt that...incredible feeling again until now.

Blinking, he continued to stare at her in the darkness of the car.

Once before, when she'd been a gawky fourteen year old, Katie had profesed her love and kissed him—right in front of his friends, mortifying him. He'd been too embarrassed to react, or even to think about that kiss. Until now.

This was Katie, *little* Katie, he reminded himself, but the message seemed to be getting garbled somewhere along the way. The woman before him *looked* like Katie, but land's sake, the thoughts racing through his suddenly tense, tight body certainly couldn't have anything to do with her. Nor could the emotions that were churning around inside of him.

He'd been physically attracted to women—lots of women—and a few he'd even allowed himself to care about. But not since his divorce. Not since he'd had his heart and his guts torn in two.

Never again, he reminded himself, no matter what a

woman stirred in him. Never again would he allow himself
to be vulnerable, to be hurt, to be made a fool of. Never
again would he care, or let his emotions overrule his intel-
lect.

Not even for Katie.

Especially for Katie.

She was sacred. She was…family. She deserved better.
Besides, once before he'd disappointed his family.

He'd been a brash fifteen-year-old, rebellious and headstrong and hurting over the death of his beloved father.
With no way to vent the pain, he'd joined a neighborhood
gang, much to his family's horror.

He would never forget the look on his mother's face
when she learned what he'd been up to. She'd been devastated, and so had the rest of the family. Michael had been
away at college, and had come home to try and talk some
sense into him. Once he realized how devastating his actions had been, he vowed that he would never, ever again
do anything to disappoint his family. He never wanted to
cause anyone that kind of pain, or see that devastated look
on his mother's face again.

Katie was family, oh, maybe not by birth or blood, but
family just the same. And if he ever did anything to hurt
her, it would devastate his mother, not to mention the rest
of the family. And he would never, ever do that again, not
for anyone or any reason.

Katie was a woman who deserved so much more than
his tattered, cold heart could ever give her. She deserved a
husband who loved her, a home, a family. He'd long ago
given up on happily ever after out of necessity, out of sur-
vival and maybe a little out of fear.

No, he would never allow another woman to ensnare his
heart.

Especially Katie.

Still stunned by the touch of his lips on hers, he turned
away from her and stared out the windshield. If Katie had

noticed his shocked reaction to the kiss, she didn't let on, he realized gratefully.

She'd noticed.

Katie let out a breath she hadn't known she was holding. She held the baby tighter, grateful for the darkness, grateful Danny couldn't see how the briefest touch of his lips had sent her world rocking. She'd fantasized about kissing him for so long, it was almost as if she had been dreaming, it had been so brief, so intense.

But she couldn't—wouldn't—let her emotions run rampant. She'd promised herself when she came home that she would never make a fool of herself over Danny again.

Danny was more than accustomed to having women fall at his feet. Like all the Sullivan brothers, women naturally seemed to flock to him. She wasn't about to be just another female in the crowd. Nor was she ever going to open herself up to the pain of revealing her true feelings for him. She'd barely survived the humiliation the last time.

One rejection in a lifetime from the man you loved was more than enough for any woman.

No, she wouldn't let him know how he affected her until he stopped treating her like a kid, and started accepting her for the woman she was.

"We'd better get going," Danny said, sparing a glance at her. "Our food's getting cold and I just realized I'm starving." The rain seemed to be coming down harder, flooding the streets and drenching what little grass there was in the neighborhood.

The moment of tension seemed to have been broken. "So am I." Katie sighed in relief, then slipped the sleeping baby back into her car seat, taking a moment to make sure she was fastened in correctly. A sudden thought had her hands stilling.

"Danny?"

"What?" He turned to look at her. She was still shadowed by a street lamp and for the first time he noticed the dark circles under her eyes. She looked beat, he realized, and felt a stab of guilt.

"If we're going to keep the baby overnight, exactly *where* are we going to keep her?" She looked at him suspiciously, her heart suddenly pounding in fear.

"Well…" he began, a grin forming on his face.

"Oh, no." She shook her head at his mischievous look. "Absolutely not. You're going to get us arrested," she muttered, not certain *what* he was up to, but quite certain it was *not* good. "It'll be klink time for both of us."

"Now, Katie, would I do that to you?" He laughed at the look she shot him.

"All right," she muttered, dragging a hand through her hair, then taking a deep, fortifying breath. The man was going to make her old and gray before her time. "Let's hear it. *All* of it," she specified, glaring at him. "Exactly *where* do you propose we stash this kid tonight?"

Chapter Four

"Oh, my God, Danny, are you out of your mind?" Katie asked for about the tenth time as she unlocked the back door of the day-care center, juggling her keys and purse in one hand, and their bag of food and the baby's supplies in the other.

He was bringing up the rear with the baby in the car seat, bumping Katie along to get her moving every time she stopped to yell at him. She stepped inside, hit a switch and the center was flooded with light. As he stepped in, still hauling the baby carrier, she shut and locked the door behind him, then snapped the draperies closed.

"This is ridiculous," she said as she dropped her purse onto a child-size table and followed him into the kitchen, turning lights on as she went. Dragging a hand through her hair, she pushed the damp strands off her face. She dropped the bag of take-out food onto the long kitchen table, followed by the baby supplies. "Absolutely ridiculous, Danny." With a sigh of fatigue and exasperation, she shook her head.

"What's ridiculous about it?" Danny asked, glancing

around for a place to set the car seat. He settled for an empty spot on the floor, near a playpen that was used for the smaller children in Katie's care. "Actually, I think it's the most sensible idea I've had all day."

"Sensible?" Katie nearly shuddered. "Nothing we've done tonight has been sensible. If we were sensible, we would have turned Molly over to DCFS by now." Her voice shimmered with anger, but her words had lost some of their resolve. The more time that passed, the less she wanted to turn the baby over to anyone, let alone DCFS. She couldn't bear the thought that little Molly might be lost in the huge system. And she hated to admit that she was falling in love with the little tyke.

"Now that wouldn't be sensible, Kat. That would be cruel." Something in his voice made her glance up at him. "Think about it, Kat. Bringing the baby here is logical. The center is closed until Monday, so that almost certainly guarantees us privacy. I certainly can't take Molly home to my mother and Da. Everyone in the entire neighborhood would find out about Molly, since you know how besotted Da is about babies." He leaned down and picked up the baby, cuddling her close. "He'd be out prancing the streets with Molly, showing her off, showing her the sights and giving us away in no time." He grinned at the thought.

Katie laughed, knowing what he said was true. "Well, you've got a point there."

"And then there's Michael and Patrick. You know darn well if they knew about Molly, they'd be breaking their backs to help us find who she belongs to. Before long, the whole precinct would know something was up." He shook his head, bouncing the baby gently in his arms. "Besides, now that Joanna is expecting again, Michael is a wreck. You know how much trouble she had giving birth to Emma. He doesn't need anything else to worry about."

"True," she agreed. "And we both know Michael has a tendency to worry. About everything," she quickly added, her smile filled with love and affection for the oldest of the Sullivan brothers.

"Exactly. And the next thing you know, the captain would catch on, and my rear would be in deep, serious doo-doo." He began pacing, crooning softly and gently caressing the baby's back. "The captain knows the Sullivan brothers stick together, and I wouldn't want Michael or Patrick to take any heat for this. It's my baby, so to speak, all the way. I'll take whatever heat there is." He paused in his pacing to plant a fat, juicy raspberry on Molly's neck, making her giggle and kick her feet.

"And you certainly can't take her home to your place," Danny continued, still pacing and entertaining the baby. "Mrs. O'Bannion would be announcing the blessed event through a bullhorn before you even got through the door." He turned to look at her. "And unless you want to start explaining how you ended up with a baby, I don't think we should risk it."

"I agree." Just the thought of Mrs. O'Bannion, the neighborhood busybody, knowing anything about Molly or the circumstances that had brought her to them was enough to make her shudder. Mrs. O'Bannion's sole goal in life was gossip. She lived on it, thrived on it…embellished it. It wasn't that she was malicious, she was just…nosy.

"So clearly, Kat, the center is the safest place. At least for the moment. It's the weekend. No one will be here for at least a couple of days and that will give us some time to get a handle on the situation while keeping things quiet."

"The weekend, Danny?" she asked, her voice rising in fear. "I thought we agreed it would just be for tonight?"

"Details, details, Kat." He ducked out of reach when she tried to swat him. "Let's take one day at a time. Let's just get through tonight and then we'll see what tomorrow brings. Deal?"

He looked so hopeful. She swore softly under her breath, fully intending to refuse him. Why she didn't, she wasn't sure. She blew out an exasperated breath. "Deal," she said glumly, realizing they were getting in deeper, and there didn't appear to be a rescue party in sight.

Still, she had to be firm. If he wouldn't be...sensible, one of them was going to have to be. There was far too much at stake—and not just his career and her center, but the well-being of a helpless baby. For the life of her she couldn't understand why Danny was being so adamant about this. She knew him well enough to know his concerns weren't about the consequences of his actions. He was a man who always knew full well what he was doing and accepted the fallout.

No, she had a feeing it wasn't the *situation* that was so worrisome to him, but the *child*. She couldn't help but wonder why *this* baby was suddenly so very important to him. Why he would risk his badge for *this* child. She had lots of questions, but no answers. At least not yet.

"Danny, you realize we can't keep her here forever," she said, pointing out the obvious, but she felt it needed to be done. "I agreed to keep her for the night to give you a chance to see what you can find out. But after that..." Her voice trailed off because she suddenly felt heartless continuing. "Danny?" She looked at him questioningly and he nodded.

"I heard you, Kat," he muttered. "I heard you." At least it would give him time to cruise the neighborhood tomorrow. Plenty of time. He hoped.

Katie quickly set about unpacking their purchases, while Danny paced with the baby. "The couch is a sleeper sofa and pulls out to a full-size bed. We'll have to share," she said, glancing over her shoulder at him to see his reaction.

He shrugged. "No big deal. When we were little, we shared sleeping bags and tents, so I don't see a problem."

"Fine," she said, gritting her teeth. Sharing a tent or a sleeping bag with a ten-year-old girl was quite a bit different from sharing a bed with a grown woman, but she wasn't about to point that out to him. She had a feeing he would find it out for himself soon enough. The thought made her smile as she continued unpacking the groceries while Danny entertained Molly.

She lined up the cans of formula on the counter, next to the box of rice baby cereal and a couple jars of baby food. She didn't know what the baby was accustomed to eating, but formula and rice cereal were generally staples in all babies' diets, so she felt relatively safe with those choices. As for vegetables, she would simply have to wait and see.

The box of disposable diapers went into a corner, and the clothing, sleeper and other paraphernalia Danny had bought was folded and piled in another corner. She'd learned long ago that taking care of children became a much easier task if you were organized.

"Danny, there's still the problem of where Molly's going to sleep. She could sleep in the playpen, but I don't like the thought of her lying on that plastic all night. We could cover the plastic with a blanket, but still..." Her voice trailed off as she glanced around, wondering what they could use as a makeshift crib. Fortunately, her center specialized in children under schoolage, so she had just about everything she needed for the emergency care of a baby. Except, of course, a crib, since she'd never had to keep one of her charges overnight. She would merely have to think of something.

"We'll just have to make do for now," he offered as Molly let loose an ear-piercing wail. "Hey, Kat," he said nervously. "What the heck's wrong with her?" He was still holding her and trying to entertain her, but suddenly she was not interested.

"She's hungry and I think she needs to be changed," Katie said, glancing over her shoulder as she set a bottle of formula into a pan of water and put it on the stove to warm.

The baby grunted and her face turned beet red. Danny sniffed the air, then wrinkled his nose. "Kat, I think she needs to be changed *right now.*"

Katie swallowed a smile at the slightly frantic tone of his voice. "Diapers are right there in the corner."

"Uh, diapers?" he repeated, as if he'd never heard the word.

"Yes, you know, those things that cover Molly's bottom."

He stood there, staring at her as if she'd just asked him to evaporate. "Uh, Katie, I've uh, never…changed…a diaper." Swallowing nervously, he looked at Katie, then at Molly, and seemed to grow increasingly pale.

Katie laughed. "Well, Danny, I guess there's a first time for everything." She shut the stove off, tested the bottle of formula on her inside forearm, then set it on the counter to cool a moment before grabbing up the box of diapers and a clean, dry change of clothes.

"Lay her down in the playpen," she instructed as she opened the diapers and extracted one. "Drop the side down first," she said as Danny looked at her quizzically. "See that little silver lever? Push on it and the side drops down so you can reach in without breaking your back. Not everyone—and certainly not your average mother—is as tall as you."

He followed her instructions, then slowly, carefully, laid Molly in the center of the mat as if the baby was made of especially fragile, spun glass.

"Now what?" he asked, looking more perplexed than Katie had ever seen him. This was Danny—confident, arrogant Danny. She hadn't realized that one squirming little bundle of joy could make a strong man weak in the knees. She couldn't help but be charmed.

"Take off her dirty diaper," she instructed, enjoying herself…and his discomfort.

"What?" He looked at her with such fright, Katie started laughing.

"You have to take off her old diaper before you can put on a clean one. But first, you have to take off her sleeper." She stood over him. "See those little pink roses running down the front? They're snaps. Open them and slip the sleeper off her, so we can get to her diaper.''

''Why the heck would they hide these snap things?'' he wondered aloud as his big hands nervously undid the snaps.

''Danny, she's not going to rear up and bite you,'' Katie teased.

''I know. It's just she's so...small, and my hands are so...big.'' He glanced up at Katie, and she could see the real fear in his eyes. ''I don't want to hurt her,'' he said softly, and something tugged at Katie's heart. She realized Danny wasn't trying to get out of changing the baby's diaper. He was afraid of hurting her.

''You won't,'' she assured, taking pity on him and trying to ignore the things the man was doing to her heart. ''Babies are much more resilient than you realize.''

From the way he was looking at her, Katie had a feeling he didn't believe a word she'd said.

Taking pity on him, she bumped her hip against his to get him to move over. ''Here, I'll do it. You watch.'' He exhaled a sigh of relief and straightened up, giving her his position.

Deftly, she slipped off the damp sleeper and T-shirt, keeping up a patter of instructions as she did. He stood over her, watching intently, his eyes never moving from the baby who gurgled and giggled and kicked her feet, lifting a hand more than once to reach for Danny who grinned like a fool in response.

''Hey, Kat? How old do you think she is?'' He let the baby pull his finger toward her mouth to gum it.

''It's really hard to tell, since babies' weights differ so dramatically. But from her gross and small motor skills, I'd say she's at least three, maybe four months old.''

''Her *what?*'' he asked in confusion, which made Katie laugh. He held up his hand, sensing an explanation of the finer points of baby aging coming on. ''Never mind.'' He smiled at the baby. ''Three or four months, huh? Then I guess she's had more than enough time to get attached to someone.''

"Definitely. A baby bonds with the person who cares for them the most. By this age, they can recognize faces, smells, even a touch. Generally it's their mother they recognize, which is why babies tend to cry or get irritable if someone else picks them up.''

"So that means she probably knows we aren't who she belongs with, right?'' He glanced up at Katie and she could see he looked troubled.

"Probably,'' she said softly.

"Do you think she's scared?'' he asked, his gaze searching hers. He didn't know much about babies, *especially* scared babies. "I mean, do you think she knows we're strangers?'' His anger at the baby's natural parents surfaced again and he tried hard to bank it down. Anger wouldn't get them anywhere.

Wanting to soothe and reassure him, Katie laid a gentle hand on his back. "Danny, she doesn't seem to be too disturbed by the abrupt change in scenery—not to mention her change in caretakers.'' She glanced up at him again. She'd kicked her heels off the moment they stepped inside and, barefoot, she barely reached his shoulder. She'd forgotten how incredibly tall Danny was, and how unbelievably small and delicate he always made her feel. "Besides, it seems to me that ladies—even little ladies—know when they're in good hands. And Danny, I think somehow she instinctively knows she's in very good hands.'' She couldn't help the grin that claimed her mouth.

Feeling a bit embarrassed, he laughed. He realized then that Katie had always had the ability to make him feel better. He'd missed that, he realized. And her. "Well, they're big hands at least.''

"Come on, let's get her fed.'' Katie picked Molly up, and handed Danny the soiled diaper. He looked at it as if it was a lit stick of dynamite, then two-fingered it and tossed it into the garbage pail across the room, making a basket.

"Do you want to feed her, or should I?" Katie asked, jumping when a sudden crack of lightning split the sky and artificially lit the room for a moment.

He grinned at her nervousness. She'd always been afraid of storms.

He'd always tried to distract her when she was little to make her forget the storm. Even though she wasn't so little anymore, he hoped it would still do the trick. "You do it. I'll watch."

"We'll feed her first, then we can eat. I want to make sure she's settled in so she feels some sense of stability." Katie tucked the baby in one arm, then walked back into the kitchen, scooping up the warm bottle.

"How do you know how much formula to give her?" he asked curiously, pulling out a chair and dropping into it. He would get the hang of this, he was certain of it. He just needed a little instruction and a little practice. A big dose of courage might help, too.

"I don't," Katie admitted, testing the temperature of the milk again. "So we'll simply have to improvise." She held up the bottle so he could see. "I've poured four ounces. We'll see if she takes it all. If she does, I'll give her a little more until she seems satisfied."

"How do you know when she's…satisfied?"

Katie smiled as she sat down. "She'll either push the bottle away with her tongue, turn her head, or fall asleep." She grinned. "Falling asleep is a real big clue she's done."

"Guess so." Danny frowned, watching as Molly greedily began sucking on the bottle, making soft, slurping noises as her cheeks and tongue worked the soft nipple. "How the heck did you learn so much about babies?" he asked, watching her intently.

"Don't forget my degree is in early childhood development, and you know I've always loved babies."

Katie seemed so natural sitting there, lovingly holding

the baby, feeding her, talking to her. It was incredible the way she'd taken to the baby, and the baby to her, considering that just hours ago, Katie hadn't even known of Molly's existence. Now, she was treating the baby as if she was her own.

Katie was an amazing woman, he realized, feeling his admiration grow. Utterly amazing. He couldn't think of another woman in the world—except for maybe his mother—who would have been able to handle this little...escapade with as much calm and competence.

He shifted his gaze to the baby snuggled so safe and secure in Katie's arms. He was reminded once again of how much Molly looked like Katie. Their coloring was the same, and they had the same delicateness about them. They could be mother and daughter.

Little Kat wasn't so little anymore, he realized with a start. She was a grown woman, old enough to have her own children. The mere thought unnerved him. He'd never thought about Katie being grown, getting married, or having her own children before. She'd always been a kid to him, maybe because she'd always seemed to need him. Looking at her now, he realized she didn't need him anymore, and hadn't for a long time.

He wondered which bothered him more, the fact that she didn't need him, or the fact that somehow when he wasn't looking she'd grown up? He wasn't quite certain.

Until she went away to school, they'd always been close, incredibly, unbelievably close—like two peas in a pod. When he looked at Katie, at times it was like looking in the mirror, they were so similar. Oh, not in looks, of course, but in all the important things that mattered: Values. Morals. Respect. Responsibility. Integrity.

All the same things he valued in life. All the things that had been lacking in his wife.

His ex-wife.

He hadn't thought about her—hadn't wanted to think about her—in longer than he could remember. It was far too painful to admit he'd been fooled by a beautiful face and a sweet smile. Unfortunately, that was all there had been to her. She was all flash, no substance. No heart.

And nothing like Katie.

Why hadn't he ever realized it before?

He thought again about the man she'd mentioned earlier in the evening. What was his name? Sam? Yeah, that was it. Why did the thought of Katie with another guy seem to twist his buttons? He wasn't quite sure, but the thought made him decidedly uncomfortable. If he didn't know better, he would swear he was jealous.

He had no doubt this Sam guy wasn't good enough for her. And he would no doubt have to mention that fact as soon as the opportunity came up.

"You're going to make a wonderful mother," he said softly, reaching out to touch her hand. He wasn't entirely comfortable with what he was feeling, but he had a sudden need to touch her, to feel some connection to her, to bridge the gap that the past few years had left. "You're an absolute natural."

Unbearably pleased by the compliment, she glanced up at him. The softness, the sadness in his voice caused a lump to form in her throat, and she prayed what she was feeling wasn't revealed in her eyes. She couldn't tell him that she'd always dreamed of being a mother, that she'd always thought her children would be *their* children. His and hers. It was a dream she'd carried in her heart for as long as she could remember. A dream she knew she could never reveal.

Taking care of other people's kids didn't entirely fill the gap in her own broken heart, or her own arms. "I've always wanted lots of children, Danny," she responded quietly, looking away from him because looking at him, at the sadness in his eyes, did something to her heart. "You know how important family is to me."

Danny was perhaps one of the few people in the world who knew *exactly* how important family was to her. Losing her own family at such a young age had irrevocably changed her life. In one swift, cruel moment her life, her stability, her happiness, had been shattered, leaving her alone, bereft and oddly adrift in a world that seemed far too huge for one small child.

She had no idea what she would have done if it hadn't been for Aunt Maeve and Uncle Jock. For an instant, she wondered if she would have been abandoned like little Molly? Or turned over to some huge, heartless organization like DCFS. The thought almost made her shudder and she clutched Molly tighter to her, wanting to shield her from the cruelty that could come from not belonging to anyone— not having a family of your own. Molly was so fragile, so tiny, and the world was so large and at times so heartless. The thought of relinquishing little Molly into that great morass struck terror in her heart.

"To both of us, family is everything," Danny said softly, still watching her. She wanted to reach out and touch him, to hold him until the shadows in his eyes disappeared. She wanted to ask him what had caused the pain she saw reflected in his eyes. Whatever had caused it, she knew it was somehow tied up with Molly. When the moment was right, perhaps he would trust her enough to tell her. There had been a time when he trusted her enough to tell her everything. Knowing that he didn't now hurt more than she'd realized.

Searching for a safe topic, Katie smiled at him, trying to get her own emotions under control. "So tell me about Martha." Curiosity had been nagging at her like an itch she couldn't quite scratch. Pausing to wipe Molly's mouth with a napkin, she checked the bottle of formula and continued feeding the baby. "How'd you meet her?"

"Martha?" Danny shrugged. "There's not much to tell. I met her about two years ago in the neighborhood."

"How long has she been a...drunk?" Katie asked softly, realizing there was no delicate way to phrase it.

Danny shook his head, then smiled. "She's not a drunk, Katie. I've never seen her take a drink as long as I've known her. Most people assume if someone's homeless they're an alcoholic. Not so in Martha's case."

Immediately, Katie regretted her assumption. She reached across the table and laid her hand on top of Danny's. "I'm sorry, I just…assumed… I just thought…" Feeling ashamed, she flushed as Danny gave her hand a reassuring squeeze.

"Don't be embarrassed, Katie. It's a natural mistake, one too many people make, though. Martha was widowed very young. After her husband died, leaving her and her young daughter penniless, she went to work as a domestic at one of the downtown hotels." He shrugged. "As Martha says, she wasn't trained to do much else, and it was an honest living. She was determined to take care of her daughter and herself without relying on a handout from anyone."

"What happened?"

"This is going back about twenty-some years, but the summer after her daughter graduated from high school, the kid got caught up with the wrong crowd. She ended up getting involved in drugs. She also got pregnant," Danny said softly. "Martha insisted on taking care of the baby, but her daughter never did straighten out. Martha hasn't seen her in about eighteen years."

"How did she become homeless?" Katie asked, struggling to understand.

"During all those years she'd been working at the same hotel, she never missed a day in her life, yet she still managed to raise a daughter and a granddaughter."

"The one who's going to be a doctor?"

"Yep," He sighed, pushing his hair off his face. It was still damp from the rain. "One day Martha showed up for work and found the hotel shuttered. They'd closed it down with no notice, no warning. She'd worked there almost forty-two years. She'd been counting on her retirement to see her through, since most of her earnings went toward taking care of her granddaughter." He shrugged, rubbing a hand across his stubbled chin. "Without a job and not much savings, she ended up losing the little apartment she had."

"What about another job?"

He laughed, but the sound held no humor. "She tried to get another job. But there's not much out there for a woman over sixty with no skills." He shrugged. "So she ended up homeless. She refuses to go on welfare. It's a matter of pride."

Katie shook her head, feeling a well of sympathy for the woman. "That's so sad. She spent her whole life taking care of everyone else. Couldn't her granddaughter take care of her now?"

"Her granddaughter doesn't even know she's homeless," he said quietly, watching as Katie lifted Molly to her shoulder and gently patted her back. "Martha doesn't want her to know. Having her granddaughter graduate from college and go on to med school is the most important thing in Martha's life. She worked hard to make it happen."

"She never told her granddaughter she was homeless?" Katie stared at him, stunned.

"Nope." He glanced at the baby bottle, relieved that it was almost empty. "The little bit of money she gets from Social Security she sends to her granddaughter every month. She's just wild about that kid," Danny said with a smile. "About four or five months ago the kid got sick, and Martha was a wreck, worrying about her. You need to understand that Martha is very proud and very independent, and she won't ask for a thing. But when her granddaughter got sick, she asked me to drive her to the bus so she could go see her. It was the middle of winter and I wasn't about to let her take a bus all that way, so I drove her, but only with the understanding that I would drop her off about a block from her granddaughter's dorm. Martha was afraid if her granddaughter saw me, she'd know something was wrong." A ghost of a smile played along his mouth. "She's something else," he said, understanding completely Martha's desire to shield her granddaughter and make certain she had a better life. You did whatever you could for family. Whenever you could. It was what he'd been taught, the way he'd been raised. The way he lived his life.

Katie shook her head. "That's unbelievable." Her admiration and respect for the woman grew. "It's amazing what some people will go through for their families." She stroked the baby's back, nuzzling her closer. "And then others seem not to care about their very own children."

"Yeah, I know," he said grimly, and she had a feeling he was talking about more than Molly. "For the life of me, Katie, I can't figure out why someone would abandon their baby." Puzzled, and more annoyed than he believed, he shook his head. "It just doesn't make any sense to me."

"Maybe not to us, Danny," she said slowly, wrapping a receiving blanket around Molly, who was dozing quietly against her shoulder. "But I'm sure whoever the mother is, she must have had a very good reason for what she's done." She glanced up at him. "I don't think anyone would just give their baby up on a whim." She kissed Molly's soft, rosy cheek. "In some cases, relinquishing your child takes more courage than keeping it." She shrugged. "I imagine it was a painful decision. The fact that she put the child in your car, in your care—well, that means she must have cared enough to make sure the baby was well looked after."

He wanted to accept what she was saying, but it wasn't easy. "Not everyone has natural mothering instincts, Katie," he said, his tone harsh, causing her to look at him curiously. "And unfortunately not all women want children." Face grim, he stood and extended his arms for the baby. Katie handed him the child, then watched as he gently laid Molly on her tummy in the playpen, before gently covering her with a blanket.

He stood over the baby for a few moments. Then he leaned over and tucked her little toy near her. He glanced up to find Katie watching him with a smile.

"Just so she has something familiar near her," he said

by way of explanation. "If she wakes up and realizes she's in a strange place, I don't want her to be frightened." He shrugged. "If she has something familiar, maybe it will help."

Memories of another little girl who'd been left all alone in the world came flooding back. When she would awaken at night, frightened and terrified, it was Danny who had been there to comfort her, to reassure her. Danny who had sat with her until the demons disappeared and she knew she was safe.

Touched by his compassion, Katie wanted to go to him, to offer the comfort he'd once offered her, but she didn't. Instead, she busied herself gathering paper plates and napkins from the cabinet, grateful to have something to do to keep her mind off her own churning emotions.

"Come on, let's eat. I'm starving." She reached for the carryout bag, smelled the heavenly aroma and nearly swooned. She pounced on a sack of French fries, greedily stuffing several into her mouth. She'd been far too busy with the children for lunch, and dinner had turned out to be an empty promise.

"God, Kat, I'm starving, too," Danny said as he plopped down in his own seat. "Got any Ketchup around here?" he asked as he popped a fry in his mouth, then grabbed two cold drinks from the bag along with several hot dogs.

Turning to the large refrigerator in the kitchen, she opened the door and pulled out a bottle of Ketchup. Since she served lunch daily at the center, the refrigerator and cabinets were usually well stocked. But today was Friday, she realized with a frown, and the refrigerator and cupboards would need to be replenished. A chore usually reserved for Saturday or Sunday when the center was closed.

Danny handed her one of the hot dogs. "This one's yours." He managed a grin. "Chili dogs from Antonio's, remember?"

Katie snatched the hot dog from him, her mouth salivating. "How could I forget?" she asked, thinking of how pleased she'd been when he pulled through the drive-in earlier this evening.

She'd always had a nervous stomach. As a child, whenever she was upset, she couldn't eat. But Danny had found her one weakness. Chili dogs from Antonio's. He would bribe her to eat with the promise of a chili dog. She'd loved them so much, it never failed to do the trick. It still touched her immensely that he had remembered.

"A Sullivan never forgets," he said with a rakish grin, digging into his own food. They ate in silence for a moment. He glanced at the baby. She was sleeping comfortably, her round little rump airborne, small sucking sounds coming from the stub of a thumb in her mouth. "Molly looks pretty peaceful," he said, as if surprised.

"She's dry, fed, warm and happy. What more could she want?" The moment the words were out of her mouth she regretted them.

"There's a lot more things she could want, Kat," he said grimly. "Like a mother who wanted her, took care of her—"

"Danny, I'm sorry. I didn't mean... It was thoughtless—"

"It's not your fault, Katie." Sighing, he pushed his food away and dragged a hand through his hair. "I'm sorry, it's just...this thing has really gotten to me." He rose from the table and began to pace, and she realized he was taking this situation far too personally.

Katie picked at her food, wanting to say something to soothe him, wanting nothing more than to reassure him. "Danny, I'm sure we'll be able to find out whom she belongs to. We just need a little more time." She didn't add that they were running out of time. Keeping an abandoned baby for a few hours was one thing. Keeping a baby for several days or even weeks was quite another. But now wasn't the time to point that out, she realized.

"Yeah, and when I do..." His voice trailed off as his fists clenched. "You know, Katie, after almost fifteen years as a cop, I thought I'd seen everything. Thought I'd experienced everything. But this—'' He glanced at Molly. "This tops it."

Curious, Katie watched him, wondering for the umpteenth time why this child and this situation were getting to him so much. Danny was a man who rarely lost his cool. So what was it about this situation that was tearing him up?

He paused in front of the playpen. His face softened, then he leaned over and tucked the blanket more securely around Molly who'd kicked part of it off in her sleep.

"She's so adorable and so helpless," he said so softly she almost didn't hear him. "Molly." He said the name with a smile, then glanced at Katie. "I love that name. I always thought I'd name my first daughter after my late grandmother. It seemed fitting somehow, you know, especially since she never lived to see any of us."

She was stunned to hear him speak of having a child. Marriage and children were something no one talked about with Danny, not since his failed marriage.

After Michael had married Joanna Grace and adopted her newborn, Emma, the family had teased Danny and his younger brother, Patrick, about continuing the Sullivan line. But after his brief marriage, whenever the subject came up, Danny suddenly left the room. No one teased him or broached the subject anymore, so she was surprised to hear him talk about it.

"Da would love it," she said quietly. Thunder rumbled ominously overhead. She glanced away, trying to gather her courage. "Danny, I, uh, didn't know you even wanted a child."

He grunted softly. "Wanted a child, Kat?" He turned to her, his fists clenched tightly in his pockets, his eyes dark and hard. The look in them was suddenly so bleak, so bereft, she felt her heart constrict. "Hell, Katie, I *had* a child."

Chapter Five

Rain pelted the roof in a steady, rhythmic pattern, matching the frantic beating of Katie's heart.

Stunned, she merely stared at him, unable to speak. Her breath hitched twice before she got it under control. The blood in her veins felt as if it had turned to icicles.

Of all the things she'd expected him to tell her, this certainly was not one of them. It had simply never occurred to her.

A million questions tumbled through her mind, crowding away her shock. But her first instinct was to calm, to soothe, to comfort—much the same way Danny had comforted her so many times in the past.

She wasn't even certain she knew how.

Danny had a child.

But not with her—not her child.

It hurt more than she'd ever thought possible, she realized. Yet it was secondary to the pain she felt for him.

Something terrible *had* happened to him. She knew it now, knew it as if someone had whispered the words of truth in her ears.

What had happened?

Why hadn't anyone told her?

And *where* was the child?

The answers would have to wait. She would have to push aside her own feelings, her own fears, her own questions, because right now there was something far more important.

Danny.

He'd walked to the window in the darkened playroom, and now just stood there, staring outside. Hands jammed in his pockets, his back was broad, his shoulders wide, his burden heavy.

Her appetite gone, Katie stood and went to him, forgetting her resolve, forgetting caution. For the first time in her life Danny needed *her,* and she couldn't help but respond.

"Danny." Gently, she laid a hand on his back, wanting him to know she was there, but wanting him to know she wouldn't pry. She would let him tell her in his own way, in his own time. It was all part of the trust they'd once shared that had seemed so tenuous and fleeting in the past few years.

His pain was like a living thing, emanating from him like waves from an ocean. Each ragged breath he took cut like a saber in her heart. She wanted to fold him in her arms and hold him, but she didn't—couldn't.

They stood in the darkened quiet for a moment, watching rain pelt the windows and drench the earth.

"I'm sorry," he finally whispered, rubbing a hand over his weary eyes. He suddenly felt very old and very, very tired. "I didn't mean to just blurt it out like that."

She swallowed back the tears that had quickly filled her eyes at the sound of his voice. He sounded so hollow, so beaten, so...heartbroken. There was no other word to describe it. Danny was heartbroken.

"It's all right, Danny." Instinctively, she slipped an arm around his waist. Comforting him came as natural to her as breathing.

"Kat." He said nothing more than her name as he turned

and enfolded her in his arms, holding her close. God, she was warm and soft, and he needed her so much right now— more than he'd ever needed anyone. His eyes slid closed and he savored her scent as the pain inside tore at him.

He'd missed Katie, he realized with increasing clarity. Missed the friendship they'd always had, missed the closeness they'd always shared, missed having her in his life. Missed her.

Until this moment, he hadn't known how much. Hadn't realized how lonely and empty he'd been—by choice. He hadn't wanted anyone to get close to him; hadn't wanted anyone to share his pain, his burden.

He'd kept it all bottled up inside of him for so long that now he seemed about ready to explode. He had to get it out, had to cleanse himself of the guilt and the nightmares that had plagued him for so long.

"I...I...never told anyone," he said softly, resting his stubbled cheek against hers, marveling at the soft creaminess of her skin and her gentle scent that seemed to lull and mesmerize. Holding Katie, he felt as if he'd come...home. He didn't pause to wonder why.

She clung to him, holding him tight, clutching the back of his still-damp shirt, wanting to absorb his pain, her heart thrumming frantically from his closeness and her own fear. She didn't speak, didn't question. She just held him, tilting her head back to look at him, hating the tormenting shadows she saw reflected in his eyes.

"I couldn't tell anyone," he went on quietly as rain beat a staccato rhythm overhead. "It was too painful. Too hard. Too devastating..." His voice trailed off and he laid a hand to her cheek. Her eyes were wide and damp with tears, and he wanted to smile, warmed by her compassion, her understanding. But she'd always been like that. Always wore her heart on her sleeve for the whole world to take and break.

For the first time in a long, long time, he felt a profound

sense of peace, something that had been missing in his life for so long. Until now, he hadn't even realized it.

"I thought I could handle it," he went on softly, absently stroking her back. "And I did. I'd managed to bury everything—my memories, my feelings. Everything." His gaze shifted across the darkened room to the playpen where Molly was sleeping soundly, safely. "Until I found Molly in my car." He sighed heavily. "Seeing that baby brought back all the feelings I'd kept inside. She's so small, so helpless...I just don't understand how someone could not want their own child...." His voice trailed off. Nervously, he cleared his throat and went on. "While you were away, I started dating Carla. You remember Carla from school, don't you?"

"Yes," she said hesitantly, trying to keep the tension from her voice as anger spurted. She remembered Carla very well. Extremely pretty and perky, Carla had been a popular cheerleader who had done her level best to get one of the Sullivan brothers—any Sullivan brother—to notice her, to no avail. Carla was one of those self-involved spoiled women who thought the world owed her something. She saw men not as partners or people, but as trophies, something to hang on her arm to make her look good. She'd made no secret of the fact that she intended to "catch" one of the wildly popular Sullivan boys. Katie had always thought it would be Patrick. She was stunned to realize it had been Danny.

"She was bright and pretty, Kat, and fun to be around. And unfortunately I fell wildly in love with her. Or so I'd thought," he added grimly.

Like his brothers, at a young age he had been instilled with the knowledge that marriage was a serious business, not to be undertaken lightly. It was a sacred, solemn promise, a pledge made before God and family, to be honored and cherished all the days of your life.

Like their parents and grandparents before them, all of the Sullivan boys wanted to find their soul mate: a best friend, a lover, a woman who would support you and your dreams, while you did the same and more for them.

As he had learned from watching his parents, marriage to the right person would enhance your life and bring untold joy and happiness. He hadn't realized how painful marriage to the wrong person could be. Or how serious the consequences.

He did now.

"About four months after we started dating, Carla told me she was pregnant." He let out a frustrated breath. "I have to admit I was shocked at first. It wasn't something I had counted on or expected. I mean, we took precautions but...I don't know. These things happen, I guess. Even though it was unexpected, I realized what a blessing it was. The woman I loved was carrying my child. What more could a guy want from life?" He shook his head, the ghost of a smile on his face. "You know how important family is to all of the Sullivans. All I could think of was how happy Da would be. First Emma, now another grandchild."

She wanted to weep at the tone of his voice, knowing how pleased and happy he must have been to be able to give Da another grandchild, to carry on the Sullivan name, which was the most important thing to Da. Family. Tradition.

"Naturally, I asked Carla to marry me."

"Naturally." She would expect no less of Danny or his brothers. Responsibility was not merely a word, but a way of life to them.

"Carla was adamant about not telling anyone about the pregnancy, especially the family. She'd had a few problems and was concerned about losing the baby. She didn't want to disappoint them. I thought she might have been a little embarrassed about getting pregnant, as well." He shrugged his shoulders. "I understood and agreed. Maybe it wasn't the best scenario, or one that I'd planned, but I was in love with her and determined to make a go of the marriage. And, Katie, I wanted that baby very, very much."

"I know." Eyes closed, she rested her head against his chest. She had no doubt that Danny would make the very best of any situation, but especially a marriage. And as for a child, there was no doubt about his feelings. Danny was born to be a father.

"Carla didn't want a big fuss or anything, so we eloped. It was odd getting married without the family there. It's not exactly the way I'd dreamed it would be. I'd always wanted a wedding like Michael's. You know, the whole family gathered at the pub to celebrate and wish us well, but I wanted to please her." He couldn't express how much it had pained him not to have his mother, brothers or grandfather there to witness him exchange his vows, to watch him pledge his life to the woman he'd planned to spend his life with, a woman who was carrying his child.

"For the first couple of months I guess Carla thought it was fun playing house. But then, she started getting bored and going out at night with her friends. I worried because of the baby and we argued about it." He paused for a moment, the only sound that of his heart pounding steadily against hers. "About three months after our marriage, I got a call at the station. Carla had been rushed to the hospital. She'd had a miscarriage."

"I'm so sorry, Danny." Heart aching, she merely held him.

"I was devastated. Just devastated." The sigh he exhaled was long and ragged. "After Carla lost the baby, she also lost interest in me and our marriage. I tried talking to her, reasoning with her. Nothing worked, Kat. She just went on, acting like she was still single. Going out every night, carousing with her girlfriends. I even suspected there was another guy somewhere." It was his tone of voice—the sharp pain, the utter defeat—that had her looking up at him, her gaze searching his.

She didn't want to see what she saw. Danny, who'd always been so fearless, so strong and impenetrable, so cocky and arrogant, now looked haunted, defeated. Heartbroken, she thought again. It made her throat constrict. She'd never felt so helpless before. Never realized how much loving someone caused you to *feel* their pain. She ached for him, and knew there was nothing she could do but be there for him, and listen.

"Let me tell you something, Katie, there is no way in hell a relationship can work when only one person is trying." His voice had hardened. "Maybe it wasn't an ideal situation or the best way to start a marriage, but I thought we had enough going for us to make it work."

How well she knew that one person caring didn't a relationship make. His words caused the lump in her throat to grow. Hadn't she spent the better part of her life wildly, hopelessly in love with a man who didn't care? No, one person couldn't make a relationship work, no matter how much they loved the other person.

"About a month after she lost the baby, we had a major blow up. I told her I wanted to know whether or not she was willing to work at our marriage." His voice dropped a decibel and he shook his head. "Kat, nothing in the world could have prepared me for her response." He looked down at her, his gaze meeting hers.

"It was an ugly scene, Kat. Very ugly. She told me some half-baked story about deliberately getting pregnant so I'd have to marry her, then she confessed she hadn't had a miscarriage, she'd had an abortion. There were some complications, which was why she was rushed to the hospital." His breath shuddered out. "She told me she'd never loved me, and had deliberately killed our baby because she didn't want to be tied down to me anymore."

Shocked, tears filled Katie's eyes and she clung to him, unable to comprehend what he'd gone through. Perhaps other men could have accepted Carla's words and her lies, and not been affected. Perhaps they would have been grateful to be relieved of all responsibility.

But Danny wasn't one of those men. Family, marriage, children were far too important to him, too sacred. Knowing him as she did, she knew how emotionally devastating this had to have been, not only for the loss of a child he so desperately wanted, but for the loss of his innocence. His pride had been damaged by a woman who cared nothing for him, his values or traditions, to say nothing of the marriage and life they'd created together. No wonder he'd never confided in anyone.

"Oh, God, Danny." She sniffled, resting her head against his chest, trying to stem her flow of tears as the impact of what he'd gone through hit her. She held him tighter, her fists curling into his damp shirt. "I'm so sorry. I don't know what to say."

There was nothing to say, he realized darkly. Nothing that could change the facts. He'd been a fool. A blind, stupid fool. His desire to make a life for his child, to do the right thing, had blinded him to the coldness and cruelty of the woman he'd pledged to honor and cherish.

He rested his cheek on top of Katie's silky head, and held on to her. He felt as if the heavy burden he had carried for so long had been lifted.

"At first I was stunned. I didn't believe her. I thought she was just saying those things to hurt me. Then I realized she was telling the truth." Sadly, he shook his head. "Kat, don't get me wrong. I'm not one of those men who wants to control a woman's body or what she does with it. I'm really not. But this was my wife, and this was *my* child, as well as hers. We were supposed to be building a life together. I thought at least I deserved to have been consulted before she did something so drastic." He shook his head again.

"To have lied to me about something like that, to have deliberately gotten rid of our child simply because she was bored being married to me is totally incomprehensible to me. She may not have wanted our child, but I did. Very much." Anguish etched his words. "I couldn't believe she could do something like that to our child, knowing how much I wanted it, how much it meant to me. Hell, I would have raised it myself. I wouldn't have held on to Carla, or used the child to bind her to me. I knew I'd made a terrible mistake long before that, and I certainly didn't want to prolong it. Why make both of us miserable?" He took a slow, deep breath, his arms tightening around her. "But that didn't mean I didn't want our child." He shook his head. "I couldn't forgive her, Kat, not for any of it. For lying to me, for deceiving me, for making a mockery of all the things I valued and believed in. Our marriage was some sort of joke to her, and I was some kind of prize." Disgust laced his words. "More importantly, I could never forgive her for what she'd done to our child."

Pain and anger roared through Katie, and she had to bite down hard on her tongue not to let loose the spew of words that threatened to overflow. Her feelings for Carla had never been favorable; now they were downright dangerous.

"What finally happened?" she asked quietly, snuggling closer to him. She needed to be close now, not certain if it was for his comfort, or for her own.

"When I realized the truth, I knew there was nothing left of our marriage. Nothing left of our relationship, if there had ever been one. The wound was too raw, too deep. I moved out that night and called my cousin Peter. He handled all the paperwork and filed my divorce papers the next morning."

Her gaze searched his. "Did you tell Peter anything?"

Danny shook his head. "No, I couldn't, Kat. I guess from the way I was acting he knew something terrible had happened, but he didn't pry and didn't ask a bunch of stupid questions. Except he did ask if I was all right, and if I wanted him and his brothers to beat anyone up for me."

Shaking her head, she laughed softly, relieved that the tension had been broken, if only for a moment. "That sounds like Peter." She didn't add that she would have gladly made the offer, as well.

Peter Sullivan was the oldest of one of Da's six brothers' sons. He was also one of three brothers who were as close as Michael, Danny and Patrick. They had spent long hours together playing as children. While Michael, Danny and Patrick had followed in their father's footsteps and gone into law enforcement, Peter, Tommy and Sean Sullivan had followed in their father's footsteps and all become lawyers.

"I just told Peter I wanted it done quickly and quietly." Danny sighed. "I don't know how he did it, but it was all over in six months. The last I heard, Carla had taken off to Vegas with a guitar player from some rock band." His smile was sad. "Guess he wasn't quite so boring."

"Danny, this wasn't your fault." She could hear the guilt underlying his words, and knew that he blamed himself. "Not any of it," she insisted as protective pride for Danny rose. She could feel her temper rising again. How dare Carla do such a thing to Danny, and leave him feeling as if he were to blame for her immaturity and callousness. "Don't you dare blame yourself," Katie ordered. "What Carla did was unforgivable, Danny. All of it. Your response was perfectly understandable under the circumstances. You had no way of knowing that she would do something like that, or that she hadn't married you with honest intentions."

"I should have known," he insisted firmly. "I'm not a naive kid, Kat. I should have known better, and I should have realized she was selfish and self-centered. But I guess I was blinded by love. But even if I wasn't, I don't know that I would have believed she was capable of doing something like that, not knowing how much it meant to me." He glanced across the room to the playpen where Molly was sleeping soundly. "I've tried very hard not to think about it, or talk about it. I just couldn't. I haven't told Da or my mother. I didn't tell my brothers, and you know how close we are."

Humbled, she wanted to weep. Of all the people in his world, he had trusted *her* enough to tell her the truth. It must have been a heavy burden for him to be carrying all this time. Especially alone. But she understood. For Danny, to have to admit such a thing would be unbearable. No man wanted to admit they'd been blindsided by a woman, let alone had one dupe and devastate them.

"I thought I'd handled it pretty well." He laughed, but the sound held no mirth. "Until today." He blew out a deep breath. "Knowing someone had cared so little for Molly that they just dumped her in my car—well, it was just hard for me to deal with."

"I understand," she said softly, realizing she did. Smiling, she pressed a hand to his cheek. "But, Danny, you have to remember something. Maybe it wasn't that Molly's mother didn't care for her, but that she just couldn't *take* care of Molly any longer. Isn't it better to make the choice she did, than the one Carla did? I'm not saying I agree with either, or that one is right or wrong, but we have no way of knowing a person's reasons or motivations for doing something. The fact that Molly's mother put her baby in your car must mean she cares enough about Molly to make sure she'd be in good hands."

"Maybe." He was still having trouble separating his own emotions about his lost child and Molly. Neither was wanted by their mother, and for the life of him he couldn't seem to get past his feelings to see the situation objectively. "It just seems so heartless," he said softly. "Every time I look at little Molly, I see my own lost child. I see what could have been and—" Fearing he'd said too much, revealed too much, he broke off and averted his gaze. He couldn't explain his feelings about Molly, his instinct to protect. To anyone who didn't know him, his actions might seem irresponsible, his feelings misplaced. But as Da had always said, some things were unexplainable. "I know it sounds silly but—"

"No, Danny, it doesn't sound silly at all." She hesitated a moment. "Do you remember right after my parents were killed?"

"How could I forget." It was his turn to touch her cheek in comfort. The pain was still there, he realized with regret. It was in her eyes for anyone to see, and probably still in her heart, where no one could see unless they really looked and listened. He'd always tried to. "You were so lost, so frightened."

Even now, the memory of that time still pained him. He couldn't bear to see such fear, such pain, in those big doe eyes. His life had always been so happy, so full of love and security. At that time tragedy had not touched him yet, so he had no personal experience to draw from. All he knew was he couldn't bear to see Katie hurting.

"I know." She chose her words carefully. "You know I love your mother and father. I always have, even before my own parents were killed. But, Danny, there were times when I looked at your mom and dad, and wondered why it was *my* parents that had been killed." Her eyes slid closed at the memory, and she felt a bit of shame, even though she knew her feelings had been perfectly normal after what she'd experienced. "I'd look at your parents, at how alive and happy they were, at how much they loved each other and all of you, and I envied you, did you know that?"

He shook his head, feeling an incredible sadness for what she'd endured. "No, Kat, I didn't know that." He cupped his hand to her cheek, drawing her closer with his other arm.

She took a slow, deep breath. Her heart was pounding from his nearness, from his touch, but what she had to say was far more important than what she was feeling at the moment. Perhaps it would help ease the pain in his heart. "I envied your whole family. Maybe it wouldn't have been so hard if I hadn't been an only child. Maybe if I'd had a brother or sister, I wouldn't have felt quite so alone." There were very few things she'd held back from Danny, but this was one of them. It was something she'd thought she would never be able to talk to him about, certain he wouldn't be able to understand. But from the look on his face, and after what he'd just told her, she had a feeling he would understand.

"When your father was killed..." She had to swallow the lump in her throat in order to continue. "I felt responsible."

"What?" He drew back to look at her, a frown slowly etching his brows. "Why on earth would you feel responsible? My father was killed in the line of duty, Kat. You know that. You had nothing to do with it."

"I know that logically, Danny. But in here—" she touched her heart "—where it counts, I thought your father had been killed because of me, because I was jealous— jealous that you had parents and a family and I didn't." Her voice broke on a sob, and Danny caught her hand and dragged her to the nearest chair, pulling her down on his lap to cradle her in his arms.

"Kat, Kat, Kat, don't do this to yourself. Please." He rocked her gently. "Wishing or wanting something doesn't make it so." He drew back again and wiped a fallen tear from her cheek. "It was perfectly natural for you to feel as you did, considering what had happened to you. Of course you'd feel a little envious that my parents had lived while yours had died. But that doesn't make you responsible for my father's death. It was part of the risks of the job. He knew that, and so does every cop who ever joins the force. Nothing you said, did or thought could have prevented what happened to my dad. Nothing. It doesn't work that way."

She nodded, forcing a smile, and shifted her weight to adjust herself more comfortably atop his lap. "I know, but I guess that's why I can understand how you feel when you look at Molly. When I looked at your dad, all I could do was think of my own dad, and wonder why—"

"And when I look at little Molly, I guess I can't help but think of my own child. I understand, Kat. Completely."

Relieved, she sniffled, then laid her head on his chest. She could hear the rapid beating of his heart, and for some reason it soothed her. For the first time since she'd confessed her love for him so long ago and their relationship had changed, she finally felt as if they'd recaptured what they'd lost. She was just sorry it had taken such a tragedy to make it happen.

"Oh, Kat, we make a fine pair, don't we?"

Still holding her, he rocked her gently, caressing her back. The dark enveloped them. The rain had finally stopped and it was utterly quiet in the center except for the sound of their comingled breathing.

Danny wanted to savor this moment of peace. Katie was so close, so small in his arms, he couldn't help but be aware of her femininity. Her scent, her softness, her sweetness. After talking to her, he felt cleansed, relieved, as if everything inside of him had finally stilled into peacefulness. He wondered why he hadn't confided in her before.

Because he was still afraid to trust.

He'd always loved Kat—hell, she was family so, of course, he loved her. But he'd always looked at her—loved her—as *family*. And she wasn't. Not really. They might have been raised together, but there were no blood ties.

In his mind, she'd always been a kid. But lately he'd begun to realize she was a kid no longer. She was a grown woman. A very attractive woman, the kind that any guy— every guy—would want. She was beautiful, loving, caring and compassionate.

Pressed against him, he could feel the gentle curve of her breasts against his chest, and the round curves of her butt against his lap. Awareness hummed through him, so basic, so primitive, it threatened to send his body into a testosterone tantrum.

Damn! He didn't want to be aware of Katie as a woman. He didn't want to think of her as warm or loving or giving. Because if he did, then he would have to acknowledge that his feelings for her were changing in a way that terrified him.

"I'll tell you one thing," he whispered softly, frightened by the thoughts rumbling through his mind. "I learned my lesson."

Heart pounding, she glanced up at him. "What do you

Play the
"LAS VEGAS"
GAME
GET 3 FREE GIFTS!
FREE GIFTS!
FREE GIFTS!
TURN THE PAGE TO PLAY!
Details inside!

Play the

"LAS VEGAS" Game

and get

3 FREE GIFTS!

1. Pull back all 3 tabs on the card at right. Then check the claim chart to see what we have for you — 2 FREE BOOKS and a gift — ALL YOURS! ALL FREE!

2. Send back this card and you'll receive brand-new Silhouette Romance® novels. These books have a cover price of $3.50 each, but they are yours to keep absolutely free.

3. There's no catch. You're under no obligation to buy anything. We charge nothing — ZERO — for your first shipment. And you don't have to make any minimum number of purchases — not even one!

4. The fact is thousands of readers enjoy receiving books by mail from the Silhouette Reader Service™. They like the convenience of home delivery, they like getting the best new novels BEFORE they're available in stores, and they love our discount prices!

5. We hope that after receiving your free books you'll want to remain a subscriber. But the choice is yours — to continue or cancel, any time at all! So why not take us up on our invitation, with no risk of any kind. You'll be glad you did!

Yours Free!

Play the
"LAS VEGAS"
Game

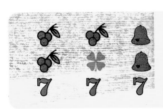

YES! I have pulled back the 3 tabs. Please send me all the free Silhouette Romance® books and the gift for which I qualify. I understand that I am under no obligation to purchase any books, as explained on the back and opposite page.

(U-SIL-R-05/98)

215 SDL CF9M

NAME   (PLEASE PRINT CLEARLY)

ADDRESS   APT.

CITY   STATE   ZIP

GET 2 FREE BOOKS & A FREE MYSTERY GIFT!

GET 2 FREE BOOKS!

GET 1 FREE BOOK!

TRY AGAIN!

Offer limited to one per household and not valid to current Silhouette Romance® subscribers. All orders subject to approval.

PRINTED IN U.S.A.

mean, Danny?'' She wanted to gently stroke his face, to soothe the anger and the betrayal she saw there, to erase any remnant of what Carla had done to him.

"The fiasco with Carla.'' He shook his head. "Never again will I allow a woman to do that to me. Never again will I allow a woman to make a fool out of me, to use me. Once in a lifetime is more than enough.''

She stiffened. "Danny, surely you can't believe that all women are like Carla?''

She certainly wasn't, she wanted to shout, but she had a feeling he was still too busy regarding her as a kid to even hear her.

"Can't prove it by me,'' he said grimly.

Her gaze remained steady on his. "What are you saying, Danny?''

"I'll date, Kat. I'm still a normal man with normal…needs, but I'm not about to ever let a woman tie me in knots like that ever again. Carla taught me a valuable lesson.'' Dropping his arms, he nudged her up, then stood himself, not liking the way his body was responding to her. It was too frightening. "I'll never allow myself to fall in love with a woman again.'' He sighed, dragging a hand through his hair. "I don't think I can. I just don't think I'd ever be able to trust myself, let alone trust someone else enough to care that much about them.''

"You trust me,'' she whispered softly, her heart aching.

He grinned. "Yeah, Kat, I do, but you're different.'' Not so different, he thought. Not so different at all. Perhaps that was what scared him the most. Irritated at himself for what he was feeling, he reached out and ruffled her hair as he'd done when she was a kid, knowing it would infuriate her, hoping it would shock his own system into remembering who she was.

He couldn't allow himself to feel these things for Katie— not just for his sake, but for hers, as well as the family. It could be disastrous for all of them. And he'd already had one disaster in his life, already disappointed his family once. He wasn't about to repeat either mistake.

The moment he ruffled her hair as if she were a two-year-old, Katie stiffened, not certain which offended her more, his actions or his words.

Different? He thought she was *different* from other women? Fury nipped at her heart because she knew in Danny's mind different meant a kid. She was tempted to smack some sense into him.

What was so different about her? she wondered. Why couldn't he see that she was a grown woman, a flesh-and-blood woman who loved him more than anything? That was the only thing that was different about her, but he was too much of a blockhead to see it!

"I see," she said softly. "So I'm...different?"

He shrugged. "Yeah, Kat. You know what I mean."

Indeed she did. Trying to contain her fiery temper, she glanced up at him and felt some of her anger dissolve. He'd been hurt, she realized. Badly hurt. She could see it in his eyes, in the lines of his mouth, his face. But it wasn't fair that *she* should have to pay for another woman's mistakes.

Yawning hugely, Danny covered his mouth, then stretched, wanting to break this stranglehold of closeness that seemed to tether them together. It was too frightening. "I'm beat," he admitted with a shake of his head. "It's been a helluva day. First thing in the morning, we'll hit the streets again. Hopefully we'll be able to find out something about Molly."

With her temper still simmering and her mind churning, Katie shook her head. "No, Danny. I think I'll stay here with the baby while you go." She flashed him her brightest smile. Maybe it was time for some...drastic action. "I'm seeing Sam tomorrow night, and I'll need some time to get ready." She rushed on, not waiting for his response. "Plus, I don't think it's a good idea to be dragging the baby all over town. She needs to have some sort of schedule. And there are some things I need to do around here before we open on Monday, so you go ahead and cruise the neighborhood. I'll hold down the fort here."

"Okay," he said, watching her. "Uh, Katie, can I ask you something?"

"Sure."

"Considering what's going on...don't you think you should cancel your date?" He definitely did not like the idea of her seeing this Sam guy, the one with all the ideas. For an instant he glanced at her legs, her long, mouthwatering legs, and remembered that she'd said Sam liked her legs. He wanted to hit something. Deliberately, and with some effort, he averted his gaze, staring instead at the top of her head.

Katie flashed him a smile full of innocence. "Why on earth would I want to do that?" She shook her head. "Sam would be far too disappointed if I canceled at this late date. We've had this planned for almost a week." She wasn't about to tell him Saturday was bridge night and they needed her as a fourth player.

Danny jammed his fists in his pockets. "Well, what about Molly?" he asked, grasping at straws, so she wouldn't go waltzing off into the night with this Sam guy. "Who's going to take care of her while you're gone?"

She laughed. "You, Danny. Now don't look like that. You're perfectly capable of handling a baby. It'll be a breeze." Pressing her hands to his shoulders, she stood on tiptoe and pressed a quick hard kiss to his lips. It lasted only a heartbeat or two, long enough to send her heart nearly into spasms. Shaky, but determined not to show it, she stepped back and flashed him a brilliant smile that betrayed neither her hammering pulse or her shaky knees.

"Good night, Danny." Smiling to herself at the puzzled look on his face, she turned and sashayed toward the washroom to prepare for bed, aware that he was watching her. With a seductive look, she turned and waved her fingers at him, then shut the door in his stunned face.

Danny stood dumbfounded, staring after her, wondering

what the heck had just happened. He lifted a hand and touched his lips—lips that Katie had just kissed. He'd been stunned by the flash of heat that seared through him when she pressed that saucy little body against his, to say nothing of that soft, unpainted mouth. He was reminded of how his body had responded earlier in the evening when his lips had accidentally touched hers.

This was Katie, he reminded himself grimly, not one of the slinky, seductive women he spent his days, or nights with, knowing nothing could—or would—ever come of it.

This was Katie he reminded himself firmly. And he had to remember that. He glanced across the darkened room at the sleeper sofa and almost groaned, realizing he would be sharing it. With Katie. For the night.

He groaned. He had a feeling it was going to be a very, *very* long night.

Chapter Six

He was dreaming.

It was still raining. He could hear it pelting hard against the roof. Eyes closed and suddenly chilled, he wrapped himself closer around the warm, decidedly female body snuggled against him.

She didn't have much on, he realized drowsily as he nuzzled her warm neck to savor the sweet seductive scent of her. He could feel her long, bare legs tangled with his. His hand skimmed over some silky material to the curve of her shoulder, then down her arm, coming to rest on the curve of her hip. She shifted slightly, pressing even harder against him, garnering an immediate response from his sleepy body.

His hand slid upward, under the silk to the sleep-warmed skin beneath, and he sighed in pleasure, nuzzling closer, planting a tattoo of kisses across fragrant, feminine skin. His thumb brushed the undercurve of a small, firm breast and he sighed again, moving closer, arching his body around hers, as his thumb moved higher, to gently stroke the small, extended nipple.

"Mmm." The soft feminine murmur of pleasure sent his pulse into overdrive. "Danny...?"

His eyes popped open at the sound of the soft, husky whisper. He knew that voice. Slowly he lifted his head. He wasn't dreaming. He was awake. And the woman he'd been— Good God, it was Katie!

Shocked and aroused, Danny leapt out of bed as if he'd been shot out of a cannon.

Katie rolled over to look up at him just as he scrubbed his hands hard over his face, trying to get himself and his wayward body under control.

Furious at himself and at her for what had almost happened—and for what had happened—his temper began to simmer. He wasn't certain whom he was angry at, her or himself.

Did she have to look at him like that? he wondered crossly. It made his nervous system practically frazzle. What on earth was going on? he wondered irritably.

The look on her face, sleepy, seductive almost sent him running for the door—anything to escape the feelings swarming over him.

Good God, how could he have let this happen?

He'd been dreaming, he assured himself. A normal, healthy dream for a normal, healthy male.

Except, he realized glumly, he'd been dreaming about Katie. And doing a whole lot more.

Not pleased by the thought, Danny realized he was having a hard time separating the Katie he'd always known from the seductive temptress who stared up at him from the tangle of bed covers. Her auburn hair was tousled, her eyes were drowsy, and he knew her skin was still warm from sleep. The soft, silky clinging number she had on was a perfectly respectable ivory nightshirt—except that it revealed everything, including the outline of two perfectly pert nipples. His mouth went dry, and he was certain that somehow a boulder had gotten lodged in his throat. And in his pants.

Unable to stop himself, his gaze skimmed the length of her, from the top of her tousled head to the tips of her pink painted toes. The silky number she wore fell just to her thighs, revealing the entire mouth-watering length of her bare legs.

Grabbing the tangled sheet from the foot of the bed, he yanked it up hard, then tucked it around her neck so every delectable inch of her was concealed.

"Cover up," he ordered, his voice gruffer than normal. "Before you catch cold." If she didn't cover up, he wasn't going to be able to get a normal breath in or out of his lungs.

With a laugh, Katie kicked her legs free of the sheet, totally delighted by his response. "Don't be ridiculous, Danny. It's warm in here." Yawning, she lifted her arms to the heavens and stretched luxuriously, totally enjoying his discomfort.

He swore under his breath as he watched the thin silk stretch across her firm breasts, then lift, revealing several inches of skin.

"What are you doing up?" she asked lazily, well aware of what had just happened between them, and how it had affected him.

She'd been half-asleep when she felt his arms come around her. Drowsy and chilled, she'd nestled against his body, his warmth. It had been a profound experience. Her pulse was just now slowing to a mere thunder, and she hoped her heart would one day slow back down to normal. She could still feel his hands, so warm, so gentle, on her skin. A delicious shiver ran through her.

Amused and thoroughly delighted that she'd finally gotten a rise out of him—so to speak—she looked up at him.

Danny couldn't stop staring at her. "The baby," he blurted. "I...I, uh, thought I heard the baby." That sounded reasonable, maybe even logical. He hoped.

Glancing over her shoulder at the baby, who was sleeping quietly in the playpen, Katie turned back to him and smiled. "I fed her and changed her less than two hours ago. She's sound asleep."

"C-coffee," he stammered, grasping at straws. "I needed some coffee." That was definitely what he needed, he decided. A good, strong dose of caffeine might be just the thing to jolt his system back to reality. A long, cold shower probably wouldn't hurt, either.

Katie nodded toward the kitchen. "Coffee's already made." She smiled at him as she stretched out a leg, amused at the way his eyes followed the movement. "I made it when I got up with Molly." She also knew what a fiend he was about having his coffee in the morning.

"I need a shower," he grumbled, dragging a hand through his tousled hair and dragging his gaze from her long, bare legs. "Then I think I'd better hit the streets." He glanced at his watch. He was as twitchy as a stallion who'd been stalled too long. "It's almost ten. I'd better get home and get a move on." He turned and grabbed his shirt off the chair where he'd left it, then stuffed his arms into it. Thankfully he'd slept in his jeans, or he would have been a lot more embarrassed than he already was. "Do you need me to bring anything back?" Hastily he buttoned his shirt, then realized he had to start over because he'd missed a button.

Katie sat up and ran a hand through her tousled hair, mussing it even further. She glanced around, chewing on her bottom lip thoughtfully. The sight made him want to groan. "No, I don't think so," she said. "We have enough diapers and formula. Just bring something back for yourself for dinner, since I won't be here."

"Where are you going to—" He stopped buttoning, suddenly remembering. "Oh, yeah. Sam."

"Do you have a problem with that, Danny?" she asked sweetly, all innocence as she glanced up at him through lowered lashes.

"A problem?" He shook his head ferociously, totally baffled as to why he was having such a problem with it.

"Nope. Why would I have a problem with it?" Deliberately, he kept his tone mild. But it took some effort.

"Good." She slid out of bed, ruffling her hair and stifling a yawn. It was a miracle he didn't trip over his tongue. "Well, if you don't want some coffee, I think I'll have some." She gave his face an affectionate pat before sashaying past him, leaving a tantalizing hint of her fragrance trailing after her. "See you later."

She waited until the back door of the center slammed shut behind him before she started to laugh. He'd looked so befuddled, so totally confounded, she couldn't help but be charmed. He'd also looked absolutely adorable, although she didn't think he would appreciate knowing that.

Different, huh? she thought smugly. She had a feeling Danny was about to learn just how different—and how perfect for him—she really was.

And she was going to enjoy every blissful moment of it.

"So there you are, Danny Boy," Da said with a smile as he drew a draft beer and slid it down the bar to a thirsty customer. At seventy-eight, Sean Patrick Sullivan resembled a large leprechaun. A strapping man with snow white hair and a mischievous twinkle in his eyes, he was affectionately called Da by everyone.

He was also the only person alive ever allowed to call his strapping six-foot-four grandson Danny Boy.

As he scrubbed the scarred wooden bar of Sullivan's Pub with his ever-present white rag, which had a permanent home over his left shoulder when it wasn't working the bar, Da carefully appraised his middle grandson. Something was troubling the boy. He'd have to be a dunce not to see it.

He felt a well of paternal love and concern that had started the day his oldest son, Jock, had started having sons of his own. The boys, as he affectionately referred to his grandsons, had grown up to be fine men. Handsome, too, he thought proudly, scrubbing an ancient spot on the bar.

And Michael with a daughter and another on the way to add to the clan. A man couldn't have been prouder, and he knew their own father, had he lived, would have been proud, as well.

"Got a problem down at the precinct, Danny Boy?" Retired after thirty years on the Chicago police force, Da still had a keen eye and a patient ear when it came to cops. Especially when those cops were his beloved grandsons.

Danny hesitated for a moment. He and Da were so close, he should have known his grandfather would realize something was wrong. He'd never lied to his grandfather, and he wasn't about to start now. "No, Da, everything is fine down at the precinct." It wasn't a lie, he realized, since no one at the precinct knew about Molly—yet.

His relationship with his grandfather had always been close, but after his father had died, during that painful, unbearable time when he'd rebelled and joined a gang, it had changed.

He'd never told anyone—not his mother, not even his brothers—about what had happened between him and Da during that time.

Out of fear or worry—Danny never was sure which it was—Da had shown up at the gang's crib one night to try to talk some sense into him. At the time, Danny had thought himself tough, strong, invincible. He hadn't needed anything or anyone—especially a family. But the moment he saw Solo, the gang's leader, pushing Da around, Danny realized what a fool he'd been, and what a mistake he'd made.

It had taken three of them to peel him off Solo, or surely he would have killed him with his bare hands. Seeing Solo lay a hand to his grandfather had caused Danny's Irish temper to flare out of control.

He'd never fully realized the depth of love and loyalty he had to his family, or how much they really meant to him—all of them—until that time. He'd been hurting so bad after his father's death that he had avoided getting close to any of them for fear they would up and die on him, as well.

That was the beginning of the end of his gang affiliation. He and Da never spoke of that night when they'd staggered home, he with bloodied fists, Da with wounded Irish pride. The only comment Da had ever made was that he could have taken the punk himself.

From that night on, he and his grandfather had shared a special bond that went way beyond familial loyalty and love. It was a bond between men that could never be broken.

"Well then, Danny Boy, if it's not work, then it has to be a problem with a woman."

Danny glanced up at his grandfather in shock.

"No need to look so shocked, Danny Boy." Da gave an offended sniff. "I'm old, son, not dead. Aye, I remember how much trouble a woman can cause a man," he said with a wistful nod. "I recall looking that same way a time or two in my day. Of course, this was before I met your beloved grandmother," he hastened to add.

Da cast a skilled eye around the bar, which was as familiar to him as his own face. Sullivan's Pub had sat on the same corner in Logan Square for more than fifty years. Located just three blocks from the Shakespeare police station, it had been a cops' hangout from the day it opened.

The pub was empty this late in the morning, but in a few hours, the place would be filled with raucous cops and neighborhood regulars, as well as numerous members of the Sullivan clan.

"So, Danny Boy, which lovely lass is giving you trouble this time?" Da grinned as he continued scrubbing the bar, inching his way toward his grandson.

Danny thought of Katie, then quickly banished the thought. She wasn't giving him trouble, as long as he didn't think of her. Or touch her. His mind replayed the scene from earlier that morning, and his body immediately responded, instantly irritating him.

"It's a little redhead this time, Da," he said with a grin, thinking of Molly.

Da laughed. "Ah, a lovely redheaded lass it is." He nodded his head in approval. Of all his grandsons, Danny was most like him—proud, headstrong, with a bit of mischief in his life and in his heart. He'd always had a soft spot for the boy. Not that he loved his other grandsons any less, but Danny...well, Danny had the temperament—good or bad—of a true Sullivan. And his grandson reminded him more than a bit of himself at that age. No wonder he was so proud.

"You know what I always say about redheads, Danny Boy—"

"And what is it you've been saying about us redheads?" Maeve Sullivan asked as she pushed through the swinging door that led from the kitchen into the bar, and smiled at her son.

At fifty-six, Maeve was still a beautiful woman. Her rich auburn hair held just a whisper of gray and framed a face her late husband had once told her belonged on a cameo. Sparkling blue eyes, so like her sons's, saw the world with kindness and humor.

"Nothing, Maeve." Da had the good grace to look embarrassed. "Nothing at all." Clearing his throat, he became particularly interested in a spot—down at the other end of the bar.

"Have you had your breakfast yet, Danny?" she asked as she came to stand next to her son. At five foot three, Maeve barely reached any of her sons' shoulders, but she'd never believed size had anything to do with authority. She had ruled the roost with a kind word and a firm hand since their father's untimely death.

She smiled up at Danny. She couldn't look at any one of her sons without seeing their father. They were the mirror image of him, a comfort in the years since her beloved Jock's death.

She had loved Jock from the moment she'd laid eyes on

him at the Puck Fair in Dingle County when she was barely sixteen. Jock had been on holiday in Ireland with his family the day they met. The moment she saw him, she'd known he was her destiny. Even if Jock hadn't. They'd had a time, they did, and eventually he realized what she had known all along. They were destined for each other. Even if it had taken a wee bit of convincing.

In the end, she'd turned her back on her homeland and her pledged match in order to follow Jock back to America to become his bride. She'd never looked back, never regretted it, not once in the forty years since.

When Jock had died, a part of her had died with him, but he'd left her their sons. She would always be grateful she'd had the great love of her life, if only for a little while. And she wished no less for her sons.

"Danny?" One brow rose as Maeve wiped her hands on her crisp white apron and waited for her son to answer. "Have you had your breakfast yet?"

"No, Ma, not yet." Dragging a hand through his hair, Danny slid off the stool, bent to plant a smacking kiss on his mother's cheek, then dropped an affectionate arm around her shoulder. "But with a little persuasion, you might be able to convince me to let you make me some."

Laughing, Maeve headed into the kitchen, her arm wrapped around her son's waist. If she was concerned about his rumpled appearance, or the worry in his eyes that he'd tried so hard to hide from her, she didn't let on.

Her sons were grown men now, she had to constantly remind herself. And she wouldn't become one of those prying mothers full of questions and opinions. When Danny was ready, he would speak of what worried him and what had put the shadows in his eyes.

And if he didn't, she would simply pry. A mother had some rights.

"Something on your mind, Danny?" she asked as she went to the big commercial refrigerator and began pulling out eggs, bacon and a thick, fat potato.

Danny shrugged. "No, not really, Ma." He poured himself a cup of coffee from the pot that was always brewing and pulled out a chair and straddled it.

The kitchen was off limits to customers, and a second home to family. At any given time during the day, you could find some member of the family back here talking to his mother, or helping themselves to one of her famous Irish dishes. This morning, though, the kitchen was unbelievably quiet, much to his relief.

"So everything is fine, then?" Maeve set bacon in a pan to sizzle while she sliced the potato and a bit of onion and slid them into another pan.

Danny sipped his coffee. "Can I ask you something, Ma?"

She smiled, turning the bacon over. "I'm your mother, Daniel, you can ask me anything." Eyes twinkling, she glanced over her shoulder at him. "It says so right in the Mother's Book."

Since she'd always had a ready answer for all their questions when her boys were growing up, she'd told them her knowledge came from the Mother's Book. An imaginary book that she let them believe possessed all the wisdom of the ages passed down from one mother to another.

"What do you know about this Sam guy Katie's dating?"

Maeve's hand stilled in the process of stirring potatoes, but just for a fraction of an instant. Aye, so that was the way the wind blew, she thought, pleased. Daniel had finally noticed that Katie wasn't a little girl anymore. She'd begun to worry that perhaps her son was going to be blind forever.

Anyone with eyes could see that the lass had been in love with him since before time. Anyone except Danny. But perhaps he didn't want to see, she thought sadly. Nothing soured a man's stomach more than a bad marriage, and even though Danny had never spoken ill of his former bride, she knew, as only a mother could, that something terrible had happened to her son.

"Sam?" Maeve mulled the name over for a moment as she broke three eggs into a frying pan, then deftly pushed two pieces of bread into the toaster. "I don't recall her ever mentioning his name, Danny. Perhaps it is someone new?" she asked, turning to her son with a smile. "You know, our Katie has grown into a beautiful woman. She is never without her choice in dates." She had not been blessed with a daughter, but she couldn't love Katie more if she were her own flesh and blood.

Danny grunted, then got up to butter his toast. He didn't need to hear how beautiful Katie was, or how many guys were panting after her. His imagination had been driving him batty all on its own, without any reminders.

Maeve slid a plate of food in front of him as he sat down, toast in hand. She grabbed her own cup of coffee, then sat opposite him at the long, wooden table. "And does her dating this Sam disturb you, Danny?"

"*Disturb* me?" Chewing thoughtfully, Danny shook his head. "Naw, I don't think disturb is the right word."

Maeve smiled. "Then what is the right word?"

"Worried," he decided. Yeah, that was it. "I'm just worried about her, Ma. You know, she's so young—"

"She is a grown woman, Daniel, almost twenty-seven years old. She's mature enough to make intelligent decisions, especially about her life and the men in it. When I was her age, I had been married for several years and was already pregnant with your brother Michael."

"Yeah, well, if she gets hooked up with the wrong guy, it would be easy for someone to take advantage of her."

Maeve fingered her coffee cup. "And do you have reason to believe this man will take advantage of her?" Her heart gave a little flutter of fear.

Unconsciously, his fists clenched. "He'd damn well better not. Not if he knows what's good for him."

Maeve tried to hide her smile. "Have you told Katie of your concerns?"

Danny scowled, pushing his plate away. "No, Ma, I haven't. I don't think she'd be too pleased to hear it."

"And why do you say that? You were always the closest to her. I am sure she would be pleased to know you are concerned about her welfare."

He shrugged, not certain he could put into words what he was feeling. "I just don't think she'd take criticism from me very well, especially about this." He glanced up at his mother. "So I was thinking…maybe you could talk to her, tell her to watch her step. Better yet, maybe you could tell her not to see this guy anymore."

"I see." Maeve bit back a chuckle. "I'm delighted that you are so concerned about Katie's welfare, but it's not my place to speak for you. Like Katie, you are an adult, and must make your own way." She rested her hand over his. "Listen to me, Danny. Sometimes when we know someone very, very well, we tend not to see them as they truly are."

He frowned. "What do you mean, Ma?"

"Because you have known each other since you were children, when you look at Katie, you see a child. Well, she is no longer a child, Danny, but a woman—a beautiful, intelligent woman. But perhaps you can't see her that way because of your past history together."

Danny sighed, wondering what his mother would say if she knew that lately all he'd been doing was thinking about the woman Katie had become.

"I think, perhaps, it is time for you to look at Katie through new eyes. To see her as other men see her."

"Like this Sam guy sees her?" He was absolutely, positively certain he did not want to pursue that train of thought.

"Perhaps." She shrugged. "Obviously, if he is dating Katie, he is interested in her as a woman. Perhaps you need to stop treating her like a child, and start treating her as a woman, too." She patted his hand. "As I have always told you and your brothers, you must trust your heart, in all things. It will never lead you astray."

"I trusted my heart once, Ma, and look where it got me."
He couldn't help the bitterness that had crept into his voice.

Maeve's hands tightened on her coffee cup and she felt
her son's pain shoot right to her heart. She chose her words
deliberately, wanting to soothe him.

"No, son, it was not your heart that was at fault. What
you felt in your heart was pure and honest. Perhaps what
was in someone else's was not. That was not your fault."

His gaze met his mother's. "So how do I know next
time if someone else's heart is pure and honest?" There
was never going to be a next time, but he wasn't going to
tell his mother that.

She smiled, patting his hand. "Again, trust your heart.
It will tell you the truth." Tilting her head, she regarded
him carefully. "Can you honestly tell me that you did not
have any reservations before you married? Did your heart
tell you this woman was absolutely right? Your soul mate?
Your other half? Did you have no doubts or fears?"

Danny was thoughtful for a moment as he stared down
at his coffee. Until this moment, he'd never thought about
it, but now he realized what his mother was saying was
right. He'd known, or at least suspected, that things with
Carla weren't perfect. But he'd dismissed his concerns because she had been carrying his child. He had been absolutely certain their baby was more than enough reason to
marry.

"Examine your conscience honestly, Daniel," Maeve
said carefully. "And you will see that whether you want to
admit it or not, there were signs. Perhaps you chose to
ignore them, but that does not mean your heart was being
dishonest, just your mind." She took a deep breath, aware
he was studying her intently. "When love is right, Daniel,
there are no doubts, no fears. It is with complete confidence
and trust that you will join with another and love eternally,
just as your father and I did, and your grandfather and
grandmother before us. That is not to say loving someone
is easy. After all, life isn't easy." Smiling, she patted his

hand again. "But loving the right person should make life easier. When you find the right woman, Daniel, you will understand what I am saying. Please, believe me. Just trust your heart, son. It will never lead you astray." She chucked him under the chin. "If your father was here, and I wish with all my heart he was, he would tell you the same thing."

She shook her head, her eyes wistful. "Remember, Daniel, for every man, there is the perfect woman. His ideal match. It is your job not only to find the right woman, but to recognize her when you do." She chose her next words carefully. "Sometimes, the right woman is standing in front of a man's nose, and she's too close for him to see."

"Did Dad recognize you?"

Maeve laughed as she took a sip of her coffee. "Not right away. But remember what I said, son. Sometimes men are too blind to see what's right in front of their noses."

"So what happened?"

Maeve couldn't hide her grin. "I must admit your father needed a wee bit of convincing, but then he was a stubborn man, Daniel, very much like you."

"You think I'm stubborn?" he asked, not certain if he was insulted or not.

"Indeed." She leaned across the table and kissed his cheek. "It is one of your most endearing qualities."

"Ma, can I ask you something else?"

His voice had changed, and she caught the hint of pain again. "Of course, son."

"How…how did you know you wanted a child? I mean, how did you know you would be a good mother?"

Maeve took a deep breath, realizing the seriousness of her son's question. Instinctively she knew that what he was asking was somehow connected to his failed marriage.

"I knew I wanted a child, Daniel, because I loved your father so. When two people love each other—truly love each other—it is only natural that they want to share that joy and love with a child they create from that love." She paused to sip her coffee. "As for whether or not I knew I would be a good mother, there is only one thing that a woman needs to be a good mother."

"What?" Danny asked with a frown.

"The honest desire to have a child. If you want a child, Danny—really want it—then that child will be born in love, and mothering will be natural."

"It's that simple?"

She smiled. "Most things in life are, son. It's people who tend to make things much more complicated."

"Did you ever consider…giving one of us away?" He realized the absurdity of his question, but had to ask, anyway.

"A time or two when you and your brothers were teenagers it crossed my mind," Maeve admitted with a laugh, then her face sobered. "I'm assuming you are asking this question for a reason, Daniel, but I will not pry. No, it never crossed my mind. But then you have to remember, raising a child is not easy, especially today. There are always problems, concerns, things you cannot or do not plan for. Illness, accidents, things that make a parent worry and fear." She took a slow, deep breath. "It's hard to be a parent, Daniel, because from the moment you give birth, your first thoughts, your first actions, are no longer for yourself, but for your child. Their happiness and well-being always come before your own."

He thought of Carla and realized she'd been far too selfish to ever put anyone else's needs ahead of her own, especially a child's. Unfortunately, he hadn't realized that until it was too late.

"So then if someone was to say, give up or abandon their baby, it doesn't necessarily mean they don't want or love them?"

Something far deeper than Katie was troubling him, Maeve realized in alarm. As she'd tried to do for all her sons ever since they were little, she attempted to answer the questions they couldn't or wouldn't ask.

"No, I don't think it would indicate that. Perhaps by giving their child up, they thought they would be giving their child a better life."

"But is that a good enough reason?"

Maeve shrugged. "Who are we to decide another's reasons when it comes to their own child? That is not our decision, nor are we to judge, Daniel. People are only human and make mistakes. Do not judge another man, or woman until you have walked in their shoes." She hesitated a moment, pushing her empty coffee cup away. "Now may I ask *you* a question?"

"Sure, Ma."

"Are you in any trouble, son?" Her gaze searched his. "You know that, no matter what, the family is here for you. No matter what the problem, together we can always find a solution. Nothing is ever as bleak as it seems when you have the support of your loved ones. Surely you have learned that by now."

Touched, Danny stood and leaned across the table to kiss his mother. "Ma, I'm not in any trouble—yet," he admitted, honest to the end. "There's just something I'm trying to take care of, something I can't talk about yet."

"And do you need our help, Daniel?"

He shook his head. "Not yet."

"If you do, you will not hesitate to let us know?"

He didn't like the worry in his mother's eyes. He'd put that look there too many times in the past. "Promise." He kissed her again. "Now don't worry, Ma."

"That is like asking me not to breathe, Daniel," she said with a smile, eyes twinkling. She gathered his plate, then stood. "You'll be here for dinner tomorrow, as usual?"

He'd completely forgotten tomorrow was Sunday. Sunday dinner was a sacred tradition at the Sullivans. No matter where everyone was, or what they were doing, everyone came home for Sunday dinner. It was the one day of the week when the pub was closed and family gathered together.

"Definitely."

She smiled. "Good. Now go get cleaned up and please put on some clothing that you haven't slept in."

He stood. "Ma, how did you know—" He laughed. "Never mind."

Danny headed up the back stairs to his apartment, thinking about what his mother had said. Maybe he could put this thing with Molly into perspective a bit better if he could just separate it from his own personal emotions and experiences. Perhaps that was why he was having such a tough time of it. He had to stop confusing the two.

Maybe he understood a little better now the difference between what Carla had done and what Molly's mother had done. They weren't so similar, not really. One had done something out of selfishness, the other, perhaps, out of love. He was beginning to understand that now.

One thing was certain, he had to find out who Molly belonged to—fast. Before he got himself into any more hot water. As much as he was grateful to Katie for all her help, being thrown together with her like this was wreaking havoc on his senses—to say nothing of his poor aching body. He thought about what his mother said, and a vision of Katie, an all-grown-up Katie, immediately flashed in his head, and he couldn't seem to shake it.

Why on earth did she ever have to grow up? he wondered morosely.

Things would have been a lot simpler if she hadn't.

Chapter Seven

It was dark by the time Danny finally headed back to the center. The rain had started to fall sometime during the early afternoon and hadn't let up since. The temperature had dropped, chilling the air, making it seem like early fall, instead of early spring.

He'd spent hours cruising the streets, talking to everyone he knew, and some he didn't, and still had come up empty-handed. No one seemed to know anything about Molly.

Out of desperation, he'd stopped at Mrs. O'Bannion's, and had to endure a serious bout of weak tea and strong gossip, but even *she* didn't know anything, which really made him worry. If Mrs. O'Bannion didn't know something, who would? The blasted woman knew everything about everybody.

Except apparently Molly.

He'd even checked in at the precinct and run into his brother Patrick. They'd gone to the pub and had a beer together, and just shot the breeze for a few moments. He had seriously considered confiding in his brother, but then thought better of it, not wanting to implicate Patrick or get him into any trouble with their captain. Patrick had a few suspensions of his own on his record. Danny saw no sense in adding to them.

Feeling defeated, he'd decided to return to the center, and Katie, wondering why the thought suddenly lifted his spirits. He'd done little but think of her all day. Like a haunting melody, she was on his mind constantly, and he couldn't seem to stop thinking about her.

As he turned into the alley that led to the center, he saw the lights blazing and caught himself smiling, wondering what she'd been doing all day.

After parking the car, he pulled out the fresh change of clothes he'd brought with him, then headed to the back door and knocked gently.

"It's about time you got back," she said by way of greeting, a scowl on her face. She'd been worried about him. He'd been gone all day and hadn't even bothered to call. After the way he'd bolted from the center that morning, moving with the speed of a bullet, she wasn't quite certain what to expect, or if he would even come back. She was relieved to see he'd apparently escaped their encounter this morning unscathed.

"Nice to see you, too," he commented, trying not to smile at the sight of her as he dropped his clean clothes onto the nearest empty chair.

She pulled him by the arm into the kitchen where she was warming up some cereal and a bottle for Molly. "So tell me, what did you find out?" She turned to look at him. "Oh, Lord," she muttered with a shake of her head. "You didn't learn anything, did you?"

He wasn't listening. He'd gone to the playpen to pick up Molly, who perked up at the sight of him. Flashing her a grin, he nuzzled her cheek, savoring her sweet baby scent.

"Hi, sweetie," he murmured. "Did you miss me?" Slowly, he danced around in a circle, making her feet kick in delight. "Really?" She gurgled lustily, making him grin. "Well, I missed you, too, sweetheart. Just as much." He planted a loud, smacking kiss on her cheek, then cradled her in his arms as he walked back into the kitchen. "How'd things go today, Kat?"

"Fine," she said, dragging a hand through her hair as she glanced at the clock. Mrs. Hennypenny's bridge group were sticklers for punctuality. "But I'm running late, Danny."

"Late?" He frowned. "Late for what?" Then he remembered, and his face fell. "Oh, yeah, I forgot. Your hot date with what's-his-name."

"Not what's-his-name, Danny." She couldn't help but be pleased by the tension in his voice. "It's Sam."

"Yeah, whatever." He rocked Molly some more, delighted when she pulled at his finger and gummed it.

"I still have to go home and get changed, so do you think you can feed her? Her bottle's warming, and I've already mixed a small amount of cereal in a bowl. It's on the table. Once she eats, just change her, and then put her down. She's been up most of the afternoon." She grinned sheepishly. "We've, uh, sort of been playing. So I'm sure she's going to be pretty tired. She'll probably sleep the whole time I'm gone, but if she wakes up crying, just change her again and give her another bottle. I mixed a couple and put them in the fridge for you, so you wouldn't have to bother." Glancing around, she tried to think if there was anything she'd forgotten.

"Why do you have to change?" he asked, letting his eyes roam over her, and ignoring everything else she'd said, but the most important part. "You look perfectly fine to me."

"Fine?" Katie glanced down at herself and grimaced at the worn jeans and oversize, faded flannel shirt that had once belonged to Michael. "Danny, these are the clothes I keep at the center for cleaning. I certainly can't go out on a date dressed like this." She always kept a nightgown and a set of clothes at the center in case of emergencies.

''Why not?'' he asked, truly perplexed. He thought she looked adorable.

Heaving an exasperated sigh, she shook her head. ''That question is too ridiculous to answer.'' She leaned her hip against the counter, keeping an eye on the bottle of formula that was warming on the stove. ''So tell me, did you get any leads at all today?'' Tension had her nerves thrumming. She'd been hoping he would come back with some news about Molly.

Hoping…and fearing. She'd become so totally besotted with the baby, she couldn't imagine giving her up.

He shrugged, still cradling Molly in his arms as he pulled out a chair and dropped into it. ''Nothing, Kat, absolutely nothing.'' He shook his head. ''It's as if she materialized out of thin air. It's the darndest thing.''

''Danny, what are we going to do?'' She snapped off the gas on the stove, lifted the bottle to test it, then set it aside to cool for a moment. ''We can't keep her here indefinitely.'' The enormity of their situation was starting to sink in. The closer it got to Monday, the closer she came to panicking. It was hard to forget what was at stake. His career. And hers.

''I don't know, Katie. But I don't think we have to panic—yet.''

''Well, thank goodness for that,'' she snapped, totally appalled at his lack of concern. ''May I remind you that we have now had this baby for longer than we can ever hope to explain logically. We can't keep Molly's presence a secret much longer.''

''I know, Kat, I know. And I'm working on it.'' He took a neatly folded bib from a pile of baby clothes on the table and attempted to tie it around Molly, who was having none of it. Making a face, she twisted her little head and clutched at the material, successfully unhinging the bib more than a few times. ''I even stopped at the station and checked out the missing persons. Nothing. Although I did see Patrick, and I stopped to see my mother this morning.''

She couldn't stop the smile that claimed her lips. "And what did your mother have to say?"

He was still trying to secure the bib around Molly's neck—to no avail. "She said to make sure we come home for Sunday dinner." He was thoughtful for a moment. "And that the only thing a woman needs to be a good mother is the desire to have a child."

Dumbfounded, she stared at him, trying to make sense of his answer. "You didn't tell her about Molly, did you?" she asked, horrified by the thought. Not that Aunt Maeve would ever betray a confidence. She wouldn't. But Katie didn't want to do anything that would disappoint her.

"No, of course not. My mother, the champion worrier?" With a smile, he shook his head. "Even I know better than that. No, we were just…talking." His mother's words had played in his head all day, along with the image of Katie. "But she said something, Kat, that made me think." His gaze shifted to hers. "Let's say we find out who Molly belongs to. What guarantee do we have that once we return Molly to her, her mother won't abandon her again? And maybe next time, Molly won't end up with people who care about her. What then?"

Katie pulled out a chair and sank into it. "My God, Danny, that never crossed my mind." Tremors ran over her at the thought of Molly being helpless and at the mercy of someone uncaring and unfeeling. A fate no child should have to endure.

"She did it once," he said. "What's to stop her from doing it a second time?" He glanced up at her, noting how pale she'd gone.

"I don't know," Katie shook her head. "I honestly don't know." Unconsciously, she reached across the table for his hand. "Danny, we have to do something to make sure it doesn't happen again." She glanced at Molly and her eyes went soft. "I hate to admit it, but I think I've fallen in love with her."

He laughed softly. "You're not the only one." He bent

and kissed Molly's cheek, shifting the baby's attention from the bib to him. In that golden moment he managed to slip it around her neck before she knew what happened. Grinning in success, he propped her on his knee and tied the bib all in one smooth motion.

"Hey, you're getting good at this," Katie commented, impressed.

"Natch." He flashed her a wicked grin. "Sullivans are good at everything."

Katie glanced at the wall clock again. "Danny, I'm sorry, I have to go or I'm going to be late. But we're going to have a talk about this—soon. We have to figure out what we're going to do and we can't wait much longer."

He sighed. "I know, Kat. I know."

She grabbed her purse and her car keys. "Don't forget what I said about feeding her."

"I won't." He stood and walked her to the door, Molly cradled safely in his arms. "Dress warm. It's cold and still raining."

"Yes, Dad," she said, rolling her eyes to the heavens and sighing.

"What time will you be back?" he asked casually.

"When I get here." Giving Molly a kiss, Katie sailed out the door, noting he was scowling after her.

Pacing the floor like a caged animal, Danny glanced at his watch again.

Where on earth was she?

And how long did this guy think a date lasted?

It was still raining. The constant patter on the roof was about to drive him insane. It was dark in the center, except for the small kitchen light he'd left burning after Molly had gone to sleep, leaving him alone with his thoughts.

He'd watched the small portable television set up in the playroom for the children until he thought he would go blind. Then he'd played solitaire until he realized what a lousy card player he was. After that, he drank three strong, full cups of coffee, which left him more wired and edgy than he'd been to begin with.

After that, he'd paced, wondering and worrying where the heck she was.

And, more importantly, *what* she was doing.

His imagination seemed to have run amok, leaving his stomach in knots and murder in his heart.

He was seriously considering calling the police when he heard her key in the door. He waited, angry, indignant, frustrated and ready to pounce.

Stifling a yawn, Katie slid her key in the back door of the center. She was certain she'd had more miserable evenings, but at the moment she couldn't remember a single one.

Irascible under the best of circumstances, tonight for some unknown reason, Sam added impossible to the list. Always a bad loser, he had huffed and gruffed most of the night about everything from the cards to how long it took her to play a hand to the coffee and dessert Mrs. Hennypenny had served. If she wasn't so fond of Mrs. Hennypenny, she would have dropped out of the bridge group. But she enjoyed the game, as well as Mrs. Hennypenny's company, so it wasn't a total loss.

At the end of the evening, she'd been left with a blistering headache and a blistering foot from wearing a pair of high heels that were just a tad too tight. Vanity, she thought with a sigh as she slipped off the offending shoe and softly closed the center door behind her.

She almost let loose a screech as a hand seized her arm and whirled her around, pinning her flat against the door. The shoe slipped from her hand as the breath rushed out of her.

"Do you know what time it is?" Danny demanded, eyes blazing with fury as he glared down at her.

Her pulse scrambling, she stared at him, perplexed. Never had she seen that look in his eyes. It was fury, plain and simple, and something else, something she couldn't quite identify.

Jealousy, she concluded with a growing sense of pleasure. He was out-and-out jealous. A slow ribbon of warmth wound through her, curling around her heart.

She wanted to grin and hug herself. The calm, cool, unflappable Danny wasn't so cool or calm now. As a matter of fact, she would have to say he was downright...agitated. It pleased her immensely.

Struggling to stay calm despite a racing heart, she blinked several times, then smiled slowly at him. "The time?" She deliberately yawned, then gently patted her mouth. "Why? Is it important?"

He slapped his hands on either side of her, effectively caging her in. "Important," he growled, letting his eyes rake over her, taking in the silky white ivory dress and jacket she wore, and the matching shoes. Shoe, his mind corrected, wondering where and how she'd lost her other shoe. Probably wrestling around somewhere with Sam the Idea Man.

"You stay out half the night, then come home half-dressed and you want to know if it's important?" He stepped closer as if to intimidate her with his size and his fury, but she could never be intimidated by Danny. As foul and ferocious as his mood was, she had no doubt he would never harm a hair on her head. Nor any other woman.

Her chin lifted and she met his wild gaze calmly. "I am *not* half-dressed," she corrected with extreme dignity. "I'm simply missing...a shoe." She wasn't about to explain she'd dropped it when he nearly frightened her out of her remaining one. "And I did *not* stay out half the night." She couldn't suppress a grin. "Just...part of the night."

In a move meant to be casual, she shrugged out of her ivory silk jacket, and watched as his eyes grew wide as saucers.

Good God! He was absolutely certain his breath had backed up in his lungs. The dress she had on was so sheer you could see right through it! It was a thin ivory silk, much thinner than the nightshirt she'd worn to bed last night. Beneath it, he could see a wispy bit of frilly lace and satin. One of the lace straps had slid down her shoulder, and the provocative sight made Danny's mouth go dry. Absently, he wondered if it had been Sam's doing.

Didn't the woman own anything with…barriers? he wondered in disgust. Stepping still closer, until he was nearly pressing against her, he let his eyes take her in as he pressed his hands on either side of her. Her hair was damp from the rain and tousled, as if she'd just climbed out of bed. Her eyes were wide and dreamy, and her lips, those full, unpainted lips that had driven him crazy, looked lush and swollen, as if they'd been kissed—and kissed well.

He had no idea why, but the idea infuriated him. All the frustration, worry and anger that had built up all night seemed to explode.

"You know, Kat, you'd better start watching your step. A guy could get ideas," he growled. "And from what you've already told me, this Sam guy has enough ideas."

Amused, she tried not to grin as she touched a finger to his temple. "Your veins are jumping, Danny." She caressed the pulse point. "Did you know that?"

"Leave my veins alone," he snapped, jerking back from her touch as if he'd been burned. "And don't try to change the subject. Where have you been?" And what had she been doing?

She yawned again. "Been?" she asked, all innocence. "I don't suppose you'd believe me if I told you I'd been…playing cards?" She laughed at the look on his face.

"Not on a bet," he growled, his gaze searching hers.

"Oh, we didn't bet." She flashed him a dazzling smile. "That would have been illegal."

"You're pushing it, Kat. You're really pushing it."

"And what exactly am I pushing, Danny?" She refused to draw her gaze from his, refused to give in to the tremors that were sliding across her nerve endings, making her incredibly nervous and unbearably aware of his nearness.

"You can't go around...acting like that...dressing like that..."

Her temper flared. "Like what, Danny? What am I acting like? Dressing like?" Her furious gaze challenged him. "An adult? Is that what's bothering you, Danny?" Slowly, she licked her lips, watching as his eyes followed the movement of her tongue. "Does it bother you that for the first time you're realizing I'm no longer a kid, but a grown woman—"

"Who seems like she's looking for trouble," he interrupted. Her words had been right on target, and he fisted his hands on either side of her head, banking down the urge to punch through the wall.

"How would you know what I'm looking for, Danny? You've been too blind to see me. But other men aren't." Tears threatened, but she refused to give in to them. She wouldn't cry. She wouldn't!

He didn't want to hear about other men. He didn't want to think about her all grown up. He didn't want to think, period.

In a move so fast it surprised even him, he fisted his hand in her hair and tilted her head back until they were only inches apart. He couldn't resist. Spurred by some force he could no longer control, he brought his mouth down on hers.

Hard and fast, desire burned through him like a lit wick. Her mouth was soft, generous, giving. He moaned softly, gentled his lips, then slid his arm around her slender waist, hauling her close, then closer still when it wasn't enough.

Her mouth opened under the assault of his and she moaned softly, tasting his frustration, his anger, his passion. Wonderful, glorious passion. Her heart seemed to soar as she clung to him, wrapping her arms around him, holding him tight, letting all the years of need and yearning pour out of her.

He was drowning. He was absolutely certain of it. He
needed to touch her, to feel that soft, silky skin under his.
His hand slid from her waist to caress the curve of her hip,
then around to her buttocks, drawing her closer still, nest-
ling her against his hardness.

It was his turn to groan as desire licked a path through
his veins, burning him from the inside out. Her kisses were
all that he'd expected, and so much more. She tasted of
sweetness and a hint of rain and he wanted to feast on her,
to sate the desire running rampant through him. He didn't
stop to think of who she was. He couldn't think. Emotions
had swamped him, burying all thought, leaving nothing but
needs and feelings. So many feelings.

It had been so long since he'd felt anything. So long
since he'd buried all his hopes, his dreams, his needs. This
was much more than lust, so much more. And he wanted
more. More of her, more of this wild, tumultuous emotional
ride. He pressed against her, backing her up against the
door, letting the weight of his body press against her until
he felt every soft inch of her, as if it had been tattooed on
his body. He knew he would never forget this moment. The
way her slender waist curved, the way her small breasts
crushed against his chest, the way her mouth opened and
softened under his. The way she fit against him as if she
was meant to be his.

His.

He wanted her, more than he'd wanted anything before.
But he knew what wanting had cost him in the past. Everything. Wanting meant losing. He couldn't want what she
offered. He couldn't want what he knew he couldn't have.

But still he wanted.

She began to tremble and shudder as his hand closed
over a small, pert breast. He heard her soft moan, the quick-
ening of her breath, felt the need that threatened to consume
them both.

Katie clung to him, winding her arms tightly around him,
letting her hand slip up to tangle in that glorious mass of

silky black hair. She could taste him, and it was more than she'd ever dreamed, all that she'd ever hoped. Desperate, all the pent-up love in her heart came pouring out of her as she pressed herself against him, wanting all of him.

She moaned softly as his hand gently caressed her breast, his thumb seeking and finding the sensitive nipple. "Danny…" The sound of her voice broke through his erotic spell. Reality slammed into him when he realized what had happened, what he'd done.

No. He couldn't do this. He couldn't let this happen.

Shame and guilt washed over him and he abruptly stepped back, dropping his hands to his sides.

Eyes wide and dreamy, lips slightly red and swollen, Katie looked up at him, dazed, confused.

"Danny?"

"I'm sorry," he said softly, unable to look at her. "I'm sorry, Katie." His blood was still pumping hot and fast through his veins. He had to get himself under control. Fast.

Tears filled, then blurred, her eyes. How on earth could he be sorry? "For what?" she demanded, refusing to give in to the tears.

"I shouldn't have done that."

"*You* didn't do anything," she corrected, hurt and furious. "*We* did it. Together, Danny. I was just as much a part of it as you."

He shook his head. "I don't want this," he said. He didn't, he reassured himself. He didn't want love and he didn't want Katie. He couldn't open himself up to that kind of pain ever again. He couldn't allow himself to care for a woman; it would leave him far too vulnerable. Especially a woman like Katie who possessed all that he'd ever wanted.

"You're lying," she said, watching the anguish in his eyes, on his face. "You do want it, Danny," she whispered softly, letting the tears fall in spite of her resolve not to. "And you want me. You just won't admit it. Or can't admit it."

"No." The word was stark, vacant. He fisted his hands and dipped them into his pockets so he wouldn't touch her again. But he wanted to. He wanted to grab her and pull her into his arms and finish what they'd started. But he knew he couldn't. Wouldn't. It was far too dangerous. He wanted her, yes, but not just physically. It had gone way past that, which was what scared him the most. He wanted her emotionally, and that terrified him.

"Yes, Danny. You can't deny it any longer. I can see right through you. You just won't admit what you want or how you feel." She lifted his chin, forcing him to look at her. "You're afraid, Daniel Sullivan. Afraid."

No button she could have pressed, no other words she could have said, would have had the same impact. Fragile male pride and wounded male ego erupted. It was as if a battle cry had been issued. The gauntlet had been thrown down.

"Afraid?" he sneered, knowing in his heart everything she said was true, and hating her and himself for it. "I've never been afraid of anything in my life."

It was a lie. He was afraid of her, afraid of what she made him feel. But he couldn't tell her. Couldn't admit she made him want things he'd given up hope of ever having. A loving wife. A mother for his children. A home and family of his own. It would never work. Hadn't he learned that? He couldn't allow himself to dream. Never again.

"Liar." She dashed at the tears that streaked down her face.

"I have to get out of here." He couldn't bear to see the pain in her eyes or the tears on her cheeks. He spun on his heel and grabbed his leather jacket off the chair and shoved his arms into it. He needed some air, some time, some distance from her and the feelings swamping him.

She stepped away from the door and watched him wrench it open and nearly off its hinges. "You can run away from me, Danny," she said just loud enough for him to hear.

She was absolutely certain her heart was breaking. She'd wanted him to see her as a woman, never dreaming that once he did, he wouldn't be able to accept it. Or her. "But you can't run away from your feelings. No matter how fast or how far you run."

Maybe not, he thought as he slammed out the door and stepped into the dark, rainy night.

But he sure as hell was going to try.

She cried herself to sleep.

As if in sympathy, Molly woke up wailing. After changing and feeding her, Katie sat in the rocker and softly sang to the baby, sniffling and wiping her eyes, and generally feeling miserable.

The baby seemed just as miserable as she, so Katie rocked her until Molly's eyes drooped like a drunken sailor fighting sleep. Kissing her sweet face, she gently laid her down in the playpen, realizing that her heart was going to be broken a second time when they had to give Molly up, because she'd fallen in love with the little cherub.

Sniffling with a fresh batch of tears, Katie climbed back into the sofa bed. It seemed cold and empty without Danny beside her. She had no idea if he was coming back or when.

It was the last thought she had before falling into a deep, disturbed sleep.

Three hours later, just as the sun was waking to spill light over the horizon, she felt a hand on her shoulder. She groaned, rolled over and buried her head deeper beneath the pillow. Her head was pounding and her eyes burned from crying. She wasn't up to facing the world yet, so she hoped whoever was tapping her on the shoulder would go away.

Far away.

"Katie," Danny's voice broke through her sleepy haze. "Wake up. I found out about Molly's family."

Chapter Eight

Bleary eyed, Katie sat at the kitchen table, drinking the cup of strong, black coffee that Danny had poured for her. He sat across from her, looking as weary as she. She guessed he hadn't slept all night, judging from the way he looked and the condition of his clothes.

Next to him sat Martha, who was lovingly holding Molly in her arms. "I didn't know what else to do, Danny," she explained softly. "She was just left at the shelter." Martha dug in the pocket of her coat, extracting a rumpled sheet of paper. "This here note was pinned to her little T-shirt." Smoothing it down a bit, she handed it to Danny.

He glanced at Katie, then read the note.

"Please take care of my baby. I love her, but I can't take care of her. I'm real sick, and I don't have any family or anyone to care for her and I don't know what else to do. I know she'll be safe here. Please tell her that her momma loved her very much."

After reading the note, Danny's heart felt heavy as he tried to understand the desperation that had driven a mother to abandon her child. Perhaps now, knowing the circumstances, he could understand what she'd done a little better. Desperation was something he knew a little bit about.

He handed the note to Katie, who read it quickly. Her gaze met his as she handed the note back to him. No words passed between them, but none were needed. They could read each other's feelings as easily as they read their own.

"Martha," he began slowly. "Why on earth did you put her in my squad car?" He wasn't quite certain he understood exactly what had happened. Oh, he understood that the mother couldn't take care of her baby, but what he didn't understand was how *he* had gotten involved.

Martha sighed heavily. "Well, Danny, I was afraid if the authorities found out about her, she'd be shipped off to one of them centers for children no one wants. Or a foster home," she added with distaste, tears swimming in her eyes. She shook her head. "I didn't want to see that happen. I know how those homes can be. Cold and impersonal. And I was afraid they wouldn't take good care of her, you know?" She glanced away for a moment, and when she spoke again her voice was very soft. "I grew up in one of those state-sponsored homes, Danny. Now, I know things have changed some in the years since, but not so much that I wanted to sentence this little baby to that kind of life. Not belonging anywhere or to anyone. Not having a home or a family to call her own." She sniffed, drawing herself up, gathering strength. "No sirree, I wasn't about to do that to her." She pressed a gentle kiss to Molly's cheek. "This little girl here deserves better than that." She sighed, then wiped her tears.

Listening to her, Katie felt her own tears well. Everything Martha had described was exactly the kind of childhood—the kind of life—she would have had, had it not been for the Sullivans. Aunt Maeve and Uncle Jock had taken her into their hearts and their home and given her everything a child could ever want or need, including a sense of family, and the knowledge that she was wanted, and loved.

It had made a profound difference in her life, and for a moment she wondered at how different her life would have been, had they not been there for her.

She couldn't bear to think about it. Until this moment, she wasn't actually sure she had really appreciated—or understood—how much the Sullivans had done for her.

And she knew without a doubt, she wanted to do the same for Molly.

Martha sniffled. "I put Molly in your car, Danny, 'cause I knew you'd take good care of her. And I was right," she added with a smile. "I see how good you are with her. How you love her like your own."

Danny digested her words for a moment, his emotions torn. He did love Molly like his own, but that wasn't the point. "Martha, did it ever occur to you that *I* might have turned her over to the state?" he asked softly.

Chuckling, she shook her head. "Not you, Danny. Never you. I know you too well for that. I know how you are with kids. I've seen how you treat everyone in the neighborhood, how you are with your own family. You come from good Irish stock, Danny. I've watched you over the years. Your mama raised all you boys alone after your daddy died, raised you right, too."

"You know my brothers?" he asked in surprise, making her chuckle again.

"Made it my business to know 'em. The neighborhood's full of information. Michael's the oldest. Heard he got himself a pretty new wife and baby girl. Patrick, now he's the baby of the family. A little too serious for me, but a good man nevertheless. Then there's your Da." Her eyes twinkled. "Like they say, an apple never falls far from the tree. I can see a bit of him in all of you boys. He's a strong man, and a proud man. I reckon your daddy must have taken after him."

"He did," Danny said, too surprised to comprehend everything at the moment.

"I knew you and your family, Danny, and I knew you'd never turn your back on anyone who needed you." She grinned, patting his arm as he flushed. "Especially a little tyke who had nothing or no one in the world. I knew if anyone could take good care of this little baby, you would."

Humbled, Danny reached out and stroked a hand across Molly's head. "Martha, why didn't you just come to me and explain the situation?"

She sniffled, then swiped her nose with the back of her hand. "Guess I panicked. When I found her, I knew I had to get her away from the shelter before anyone else discovered her. I didn't know what else to do. It's not like I got a fancy place I can take her to. I went down to the police station to talk to you, but I didn't want to go in, didn't want to be seen with the baby, figuring too many people would notice someone like me with her and start asking questions. When I spotted your car, I figured that was the answer." She shrugged. "I slid her into the front seat, then rolled down the window so she'd have some air, and then I hid around the corner until you came out just to make sure she'd be fine. Once I saw you, I knew I didn't have nothing else to worry about."

"Why didn't you tell me all this the night Katie and I drove you to the shelter?" He thought about all the running around they'd been doing, trying to find Molly's family. Thought about all the worry he'd put Katie through, knowing they were stretching if not breaking a whole bunch of rules. In spite of everything, though, he found it hard to be annoyed with Martha. Her intentions were honorable, even if her methods had been a bit skewed.

"Thought about it," Martha admitted. "But once I saw how you and Katie here were with the baby, I knew I'd made the right decision. I figured if you realized Molly didn't have anyone, you'd keep her."

Sighing, Danny dragged a hand through his hair. Everything Martha had said made sense, except for one little thing. He didn't have a legal right to keep Molly.

"Martha." He took her free hand and held it in his own. "I can't just keep her."

She looked startled. "Why not?" Her gaze searched his and he could see the fear and worry in them. "It says right here in this note that her momma is sick and can't take care of her. The woman ain't got no one else. If she did, she wouldn't have just left her baby at the shelter. So why can't you just keep her?"

Danny sighed again. How was he going to get Martha to understand that finding a baby wasn't like finding a...wallet. You couldn't just keep it because it didn't appear to belong to anyone, or because the owner no longer wanted it. Although, at the moment, he desperately wished it were that easy.

"Because I'm a cop, Martha. I'm legally required to report an abandoned child." He gentled his voice, hoping to make her understand a situation he wasn't certain he understood.

"But she's not abandoned," the older woman protested mildly, hugging Molly tighter. "She's got you." Her gaze shifted. "And Katie. Ain't that right, Katie?"

Martha's eyes pleaded with her, and Katie nodded, unable to stop herself.

Everything Danny said was true and made sense, but so had everything Martha said. Katie realized she was far too attached to Molly now to just turn her over to some agency, not knowing what would become of her. The mere idea was enough to tear her heart in two. She knew all too well what it felt like to feel abandoned, alone, unloved. She could never willingly sentence another child to that, especially one so young.

So what were they going to do now? she wondered. She wasn't certain, but one thing she did know—she couldn't turn Molly over to DCFS. She just couldn't.

What the hell? In for a pound. In for a penny. So she would adapt to wearing prison stripes. A baby's life hung in the balance here, and some things were far more important than rules and regulations.

Or prison stripes.

"You're right, Martha." Katie reached across and patted the older woman's hand. "I love Molly as if she were my own." It was true, she realized. Molly had captured her heart, and it wasn't just her circumstances, but the baby herself. How could she not love this beautiful little girl who so desperately needed her love?

"So then you'll keep her?" Martha asked hopefully, eyes wide as her gaze shifted from Katie to Danny.

They exchanged nervous glances.

"Danny," Katie began slowly, her mind mulling over an idea. "I *am* a duly licensed agency of DCFS, which means I not only represent them in a true legal sense, but I'm also fully qualified to handle all DCFS wards. So technically, by having Molly here, you *have* turned her over to DCFS's care."

She glanced at Martha's confused face and explained. "Because there are so few foster homes available, especially for babies, my day-care is licensed to take in wards of DCFS. I handle emergency cases all the time."

A grin slid slowly across Danny's face. He was beginning to like Katie's logic.

"I see where you're going with this, Kat." His grin widened. "And I like it. A lot. At least it might buy us some time." Time he needed to think this through carefully. There were so many things to consider. Whatever decision he made could affect Molly's future for the rest of her life, and he didn't want to make such an enormous decision without considering every angle. "I have a feeling Peter might be able to help us figure out how to go about this thing in a logical, legal manner." Having a cousin who was a lawyer certainly came in handy at times.

"So you'll keep Molly, then?" Martha asked hopefully, glancing from one to the other.

"For the moment," Danny agreed with a relieved sigh, hoping against hope that all the officials in this scenario were going to buy Katie's logic. At least long enough for him to figure out what he was going to do.

It wasn't his feelings for Molly that were in doubt. There was no question he loved her and was more than capable of taking care of her financially, emotionally and every other way. No, what worried him was that there was so much beyond his control.

"So what do we do now?" Martha asked, stroking Molly's cheek.

Danny glanced at Katie. Their gazes met, held, clung. She looked almost as shell-shocked as he did. There were shadows of worry under her eyes, and he felt a wave of guilt, knowing he'd put them there. And her eyes were swollen and red rimmed, no doubt because she'd been up crying after the way he'd stormed out of here last night. He couldn't think about that now. Couldn't think about the feelings and emotions she'd aroused in him. Not now, not with the specter of everything else facing him.

Right now, what he needed to do was buy some time, for all of them.

"I think what we should do is go to Sunday dinner," Danny finally said. Standing, he grinned, holding out his arms for Molly, who'd fallen asleep in Martha's arms. "I promised my mother we wouldn't be late."

Home. Yep, that was what he needed to put all of this in perspective. His family never failed to give him the calm and the strength to make whatever decisions were necessary.

"You go on without me," Martha said, shuffling to her feet and handing the baby over to Danny. "I can't disrespect your mother's house on Sunday by going there looking like this." Self-consciously, she rubbed a hand down her rumpled coat.

Danny laughed for the first time that day. "I guarantee you, Martha, no one in the Sullivan house is even going to give your clothing a passing glance."

Being a female, Katie understood Martha's embarrassment and got to her feet. "Danny, you take Molly and go on ahead. Martha and I will meet you there in a little bit."

"And where are you two going?" he asked suspiciously. He'd had enough shocks for one day. For a lifetime, actually.

"We've got a few stops to make." She smiled at the older woman and held out her hand. "Don't we, Martha?"

Sunday dinner at the Sullivans was a family tradition. It was the one day of the week when the pub remained closed, giving everyone time to spend with the family.

Guests were always welcome at the Sullivans, and there was always plenty of food and conversation to fill the large, long oak dining room table that had been continually extended to accommodate the growing family.

Da, as usual, sat at the head, while Michael and his wife, Joanna, sat on one side, with Patrick to the left of them. On the other side was Danny and Katie's place, and a high chair for one-year-old Emma, Michael and Joanna's little girl. As his first grandchild, Da insisted she be seated right next to him.

Maeve sat at the opposite end, keeping a watchful eye on her brood, and the platters and bowls of food.

From the moment Danny walked in with little Molly in tow, the entire family was smitten. In short order, Danny explained the situation. No one in the family was surprised about Danny showing up for Sunday dinner with a wayward baby. Over the years, the family had gotten used to Danny bringing home strays of all sizes and varieties. But they all laughingly agreed that little Molly was much preferred to the one-earred snarling beagle who had bitten Da's toe.

"Hand the little lass over here," Da ordered, pushing

Maeve out of the way with a good-natured jab. "A little red-haired lass, is it, Danny?" Pleased, Da beamed at the little tyke. "You're a darling, aren't you, lassie?" Da cooed, totally besotted by Molly's bright blue eyes and flaming red hair. He glanced at Danny. "Boy, are you sure she's not a Sullivan?" His eyes twinkled mischievously. "She's got our eyes." He nodded in approval. "She's definitely got the Sullivan eyes."

Laughing, Danny passed a large, overflowing bowl of Irish stew to his mother. "Da, I guarantee you, she's not a Sullivan." He held up his hands in supplication. "I'm totally innocent on that score."

"Pity," Da said, meaning it. He glanced at his granddaughter, Emma, then his gaze shifted to Joanna and her bulging belly. "We need a few more babies around here, don't we, Maeve?" Laughing, he leaned over and pecked Emma on top of her red head. "We definitely need more babies." He glanced at Patrick and Danny. "You boys better get busy. Time's awasting and you're not getting any younger." He nodded toward his oldest grandson. "Michael here is already one up on you, and pulling ahead faster by the minute." It pleased him to no end to watch his clan grow.

Joanna Sullivan, Michael's wife of a year, placed a protective hand across her belly. Just yesterday, Dr. Summers had told her the sex of the new baby. *Babies,* she mentally corrected with a smile, still trying to get used to the idea. She hadn't even told Michael the wondrous news yet. She wanted to wait until the whole family was together, knowing how pleased they all would be.

She glanced around the table at the family, *her* family, and was filled with an unbelievable wealth of joy and love.

She smiled at Da. "Well, Da, since you'd like a few more babies…" She let her voice trail off as conversation came to a standstill and all eyes turned to her. Her grin widened and she reached for Michael's hand, holding it tightly.

"What? What's wrong?" She could see the worry in his eyes and wanted to reach out and smooth his brow. Dear Michael. He was always worrying about something, especially her.

"Now, Michael, it's nothing to worry about—"

"Oh, Lord," he moaned, shaking his head. "The last time you told me that, you were in labor. Two months early." He didn't want to think of that terrifying time. He'd thought he would lose her and the baby he'd come to love as his own.

"It's not anything like that." Joanna hesitated, aware that everyone was waiting. "It's just that Dr. Summers seems to think we're not having a baby—"

"Not having a baby?" Michael thundered, his eyes going wide. "Has the man taken leave of his senses?" He glanced at her bulging belly. "All he has to do is look at you and he can see—"

"Michael," she interrupted. "We're not having *a* baby…" She hesitated and gave Michael a helpless smile. "We're not even having…two babies." She heard Patrick's groan from across the table and grinned. "It seems as if we're having…three babies, Michael."

He went white as the moon, and for a moment looked as if he might faint. "Triplets?" he fairly croaked. "We're…we're having…triplets?"

Maeve grinned, coming around the table to kiss her daughter-in-law. "Seems to me Joanna's the one who's having these babies, Michael," she said in her no-nonsense way, giving her stunned son an encouraging pat on the shoulder.

Laughing, Da slapped the table. "Three babies at once. Triply blessed. You old son of a gun, Michael. I knew you had it in you." Pleased, he slapped the table again, making Emma cry and Molly grin. Immediately contrite, Da picked Emma up and cradled her in his other arm. "I'm sorry, love. I didn't mean to scare you. But you're going to have brothers or sisters. Isn't that grand, lass? Isn't it grand, indeed?'' He glanced at Joanna, his eyes shining with love. ''Probably both,'' he said hopefully and Joanna merely grinned, shaking her head.

''Nope, Da. Sorry. Not this time. Looks like we've got a matched set.''

''A…matched…set?'' Michael repeated slowly. He searched Joanna's face and almost groaned. ''Girls? We're going to have three daughters?'' Visions of makeup, hair spray, frilly prom dresses and wedding gowns danced through his head. Followed immediately by the vision of a pack of panting, drooling boys.

He would kill them, he decided immediately. He would kill any boy who even dared look at one of his darling daughters.

His daughters.

His heart felt as if it would burst with love. He leaned across the table and kissed Joanna soundly on the mouth. ''Three more daughters? I love it.'' And he did, he realized. He truly did.

Joanna figured she'd let him carry on long enough. ''Michael…''

The one word stopped him in his tracks.

''What?'' His worried gaze searched hers.

''I'm sorry to disappoint you, Michael, but they're boys. All boys.''

''Boys?'' he repeated weakly, his gaze shifting to his two grinning brothers. He groaned softly.

''Just think, Mikey,'' Patrick said, grabbing a roll from the basket being passed in front of him. ''Now you'll know what Ma and Da had to put up with all these years.'' He grinned at Danny. ''Three more boys. Just like us.''

Groaning again, Michael hung his head in his hands. Three little boys. It was payback, he just knew it. Payback and punishment for all the trouble he and his brothers had caused his mother all these years. ''I don't think I'm old enough to have three boys,'' he said grimly, realizing he was thrilled in spite of himself.

"Hi, everyone." Katie sailed into the room, pulling Martha by the hand, interrupting the melee. They'd managed to make a few stops before coming to the house.

For starters, Katie had taken Martha to Mrs. Hennypenny's. She judged and judged correct that Martha and Mrs. Hennypenny were about the same size, and after she quickly explained the situation, Mrs. Hennypenny was more than happy to lend Martha an outfit to wear, although Martha did refuse to part with her snazzy, dazzling red shoes. After Mrs. Hennypenny's, they'd stopped at Katie's so Martha could shower, wash her hair and change.

The woman who now stood nervous and awkward in the doorway of the Sullivan's dining room, wearing a simple navy-and-white knit dress, with her short cap of lustrous silvery hair, didn't resemble the same woman Danny had sat talking to just a few short hours ago.

Except of course for her dazzling red shoes.

His startled gaze shifted from Katie to Martha, then back again. His heart softened at the sight of Katie, and all the unwanted emotions he'd been trying to ignore bubbled to the surface once again, nearly swamping him.

Here, surrounded by family, surrounded by a sense of peace and belonging, he realized what he felt for Katie could no longer be dismissed. It frightened him. He couldn't have these feelings for her, feelings that seemed so right, so perfect. Feelings he'd promised himself he would never have again for a woman. He'd vowed never to be that vulnerable again.

A spear of fear streaked through him when he realized that somehow it had happened. He was vulnerable. Caring for Katie had made him incredibly vulnerable.

And it scared the daylights out of him.

For the first time he was seeing her through new eyes. She wasn't just Katie, part of the family. She was suddenly Katie, a beautiful, desirable, incredible woman.

Somehow when he wasn't looking, she had snuck into the private little space inside his heart. No other woman he knew would have been able to handle all that had happened to them the past few days. Katie had, and he suddenly realized what an incredible woman she really was.

He couldn't handle it. Not now. Not with everything else. A spurt of panic shot through him. Maybe he couldn't deny his feelings any longer, but he could ignore them. He had to ignore them.

Deliberately pushing back the emotions that had risen so quickly to the surface, Danny rose and went to Katie and Martha, quickly making introductions.

"You made a wise decision here, Martha," Da said with an approving nod of his head. "The Sullivans are just what this little lass needs." With a little help from Danny, Da plopped Emma back in her high chair. "Where's Maeve?" he asked, glancing around the table with a frown.

"Right here, Da," she said, coming into the room with another steaming bowl of food. She smiled at Martha and passed her a plate. "Danny, go get the cradle for Molly."

No one in the family had to ask what cradle. It was a Sullivan family legend, brought from Ireland and passed down from one generation to the next.

"Where is it, Ma?"

Maeve set down the bowl, then wiped her hands on her apron. "It's in the back bedroom, covered in plastic. It'll need a quick dusting, but I think it should be fine. We can rest Molly in it while we eat." Smiling, she passed a platter of chicken to Martha. "I'm glad that you could join us for dinner. And Da's right," she said her eyes twinkling. "The Sullivans are just what Molly needs."

By the time Danny returned with the cradle, conversation had resumed and everyone seemed to be talking at once. He stood in the doorway for a moment and glanced around the table. It wasn't often he took the time to stop and appreciate his family. But now, standing here, watching them, he felt a swell of pride, of love.

Da, so happy and jovial, was the backbone of their family. Always as calm as a sequoia in a storm. Everything had started with him. It was Da who had instilled in them all of the pride of their heritage, their name, their clan and one another.

And his mother, who had weathered so much, was still as beautiful as the day she'd married his father.

He gazed at his brothers Patrick and Michael. They were as close as brothers could be, and he had no idea what he would ever do without them.

Then there was Joanna and little Emma. Related by marriage, but family still the same. His gaze shifted to Katie and lingered. She was holding Molly in one arm, laughing at something Patrick had said. She looked so natural holding a baby in her arms, sitting at the family table.

His baby, he realized, feeling a sudden rush of love for Molly. With a few prayers and more than a little luck, Molly would soon be his.

His daughter.

His child.

He could never replace the child he'd lost, but that didn't mean he couldn't accept and love a child in his life, a child who needed him just as much as he needed her.

All of his protective instincts rose and he felt a well of love for little Molly. He watched her for a moment before his gaze was inexplicably drawn to Katie again.

She was holding his child.

Until this moment, he hadn't realized how much it mattered to see Katie holding his child.

Watching her, he realized just how much of his world she'd always been. No matter what the problem or circumstance, Katie was always there, always the one he could count on.

With a sigh, he set down the cradle, running his hand reverently over it, feeling the history—the tradition—of all the Sullivans who had come before him. Love radiated from the fine, hand-carved wood, and he could feel it surround him like a warm, familiar blanket.

Family. He glanced around the table. Love and family

were the backbone of the Sullivans. Until this moment he hadn't realized how much he longed to continue the traditions he'd learned from birth. To have a family of his own. He glanced at Katie, realizing that when he thought of a wife and children of his own, she was always in the picture. Maybe she'd always been there, but he'd just never seen it.

He didn't know that he wanted to see it now.

He approached the table and reached for Molly, needing to hold something in his arms, fearing he would do something foolish and reach for Katie instead. Gently, he laid the baby down in the cradle, and gave a gentle push to set it rocking.

He couldn't deny that he was confused. Not about Molly—that issue was settled in his mind. First thing tomorrow morning, he was going to see his cousin Peter to find out what legal steps he had to take to get custody of the baby…and get the adoption ball rolling.

No, his confusion came from inside, from his reactions and his feelings. And he was not a man who liked to be confused. His gaze drifted to Katie again, and he was startled to discover she was watching him.

Their eyes met and held, and an invisible signal seemed to pass between them, something far too deep and too strong to ignore, only adding to his confusion.

Ignore it, he cautioned himself. It would only bring trouble. And he was a man who'd already had more than enough trouble in his life, especially female trouble. He would ignore his feelings until they passed, and surely they would. All of his confusion was probably brought on by the closeness he and Katie had shared the past few days and the circumstances with Molly. Molly had brought up old memories and remembered pains, reminding him of what he'd almost had and lost. He'd vowed he'd never again go there.

He couldn't. It was far too intimidating; too frightening to be overwhelmed with feelings of wanting, wanting something so badly, so desperately, it consumed your thoughts, your time, your life.

Wanting like that only brought disappointment. Not everyone was meant to have the fairy tale, the happily-ever-after. Hadn't history proven that to him?

Given time, he was certain his feelings for Katie would fade. They were no doubt merely a reaction to circumstances.

Yeah, that was it. A reaction to the circumstances. Time was just what he needed to put things in their rightful perspective.

When a man was confounded by a woman, time was just what the doctor ordered to put things in perspective. It had never failed him yet.

Feeling more confident, Danny sat down at the table, satisfied he had the problem and his feelings under control.

After all, time was on his side.

Chapter Nine

Apparently neither time, nor anything else, was on his side, Danny decided with little humor less than a month later.

"Peter, this is ridiculous," he fumed as he paced the length of his cousin's law office. "It's been almost thirty days and we're no further ahead than we were a month ago." Absently, he glanced at his watch. "Time's running out. The judge's order expires in exactly three days."

Patient, Peter leaned his long frame back in his chair and templed his fingers. "Danny, I told you this was going to be an uphill battle." Sitting forward, he splayed his fingers over the mass of paperwork on his desk and smiled calmly. "The judge granted Katie temporary emergency custody of Molly for thirty days based on her DCFS licensing. As part of that order, we agreed to try to find the birth mother." He sighed. "I've had two of my best investigators on this full-time, Danny, but so far they've come up with nothing."

"She couldn't have just disappeared into thin air."

"I agree," Peter said slowly. "But a child cannot be put up for adoption unless her natural parents are either notified or nullified, either through death or through voluntary forfeiture.''

"More legal mumbo jumbo," Danny said in disgust, dragging his hand through his hair.

Peter laughed. "Now you know how I feel when you and your brothers start talking cop lingo."

"We've only got three more days," Danny reminded him grimly. The thought caused an icy fist of fear to twist his heart. The past month, both he and Katie had bonded with the baby—bonded in a way that had nothing to do with blood ties, and everything to do with love and heart ties.

He knew neither one of them would be able to give her up. Not now. Not ever. It worried him. Immensely. As did his feelings for Katie, which rather than diminishing with time had only seemed to grow and deepen, causing him further stress and confusion. Something he didn't need right now. He pushed those thoughts to the back of his mind for the moment.

"What happens if we can't find the birth mother? If we can't get her permission to adopt Molly?"

"Danny, I told you from the start that finding the birth mother was a long shot." He shrugged. "We don't have much to go on."

"I know." Disgusted, he dropped into a chair facing Peter's enormous desk. "So what do we do when the thirty days are up?"

Peter was thoughtful. "Well, we've got a couple of options. First, we can petition the court to renew the emergency custody order. Or, we can ask that Katie be certified as a foster parent based on her DCFS licensing, which should cut a great deal of red tape. Then we ask for her to be granted custody on a permanent basis." Peter sat forward. "If we try to get you certified as a foster parent, Danny, that could take up to sixty days—maybe longer. And they might insist Molly be placed in a properly licensed home or facility in the interim—something we have to avoid. Because once she's placed elsewhere, it will be difficult, if not impossible, to get her back." He nodded thoughtfully. "I think going with Katie on this is the most obvious solution."

"Will a judge do it? I mean, certify her as a foster parent so we can have permanent custody?"

"Danny," Peter began slowly, choosing his words carefully. "I'm not sure Katie will qualify as a foster parent, even on an emergency basis."

Instantly defensive, Danny's temper reared up. "And why not? She has more experience with kids than anyone I know, not to mention an abundance of love, patience and understanding. Why the hell wouldn't a judge certify her as a foster parent?" He couldn't think of anyone more qualified to be a mother than Katie—nor anyone else he would rather have as the mother of his child.

Peter banked a smile. "It really has nothing to do with Katie's qualifications, Danny. The courts always prefer to place a child—especially a baby—in a nuclear family. Katie's not married, and even though we're nearing the twenty-first century, judge's frown on putting children in single-parent homes, especially when that single parent has a full-time career. There's always a question of whether or not a two-parent home is available, and if it is..." He shrugged, letting his words trail off.

"That's the most ridiculous thing I've ever heard," Danny snapped. "Don't forget I'm part of this scenario."

"I understand that, Danny, but how do you suppose we explain to a judge that you want to adopt Molly, but you want Katie to have temporary custody, and neither of you are married, not even to each other."

"Do you have to be so logical?" Danny questioned dully, realizing how ludicrous the facts of this situation sounded. "I don't see what a marriage license has to do with someone's ability to love a child. Lots of single people are wonderful parents. Look at my mother, and your father."

In an ironic twist of fate, Peter and his brothers had lost their mother at a young age.

"You don't have to sell me on single parents, Danny."

Scrubbing his hands across his face, Danny sighed. He felt as if the weight of the world was on his shoulders. "Peter, I'm getting desperate here. I can't give up Molly. I simply can't." The thought of losing another child he loved was nearly incomprehensible to him, bringing up old aches, old wounds and opening new ones.

"Danny, have you considered getting married?" Peter asked carefully.

The question hung loud and heavy in the air for a long, strained moment. To no one would Danny admit that he'd been entertaining fantasies of what it would be like to be married…to Katie. To have her as his wife and the mother of his children. Not just Molly, but the children they would create together.

But that was all it was—a fantasy. It was too far out of the realm of possibility. He couldn't risk his heart. Nor could he risk the relationship he now had with Katie. He couldn't risk losing her if things didn't work out. She meant far too much to him. More importantly, he couldn't risk hurting her. Ever. Not for anything.

He wasn't quite sure when he'd stopped thinking of Katie as family, and started thinking of her as a desirable woman. A long time ago, probably, but he'd been too stubborn to admit it.

He'd always thought his family could meet his needs and fill all the emptiness inside of him. As long as he considered Katie family, he felt safe.

Now, everything seemed to have changed.

He still needed his family, and always would, but he realized there were needs and desires his family couldn't meet.

He needed more.

He needed Katie.

The past month he'd been absolutely certain his emotions would right themselves and he would be back on firm footing again.

He'd been wrong, he realized, and foolishly naive. Time

was great for boiling eggs or awaiting a birth, but it had little to do with diminishing feelings.

If anything, the past month they'd grown closer than ever, closer than he'd ever been to anyone. They'd spent almost every waking moment together. On the outside, it looked as if he was doing it for Molly's sake, and he was. But he was also doing it for him. Just the sight of Katie brought a smile to his face and a lightness to his aching heart. He'd never realized before how one person could change and alter your life. How they could make you feel complete, whole…happy.

It scared him to death.

"Danny? Did you hear me?" Peter was looking at him curiously.

"I was already married," he reminded his cousin grimly. "You handled the divorce, remember?"

"Vividly," Peter replied just as grimly. "But not all marriages end badly." Smiling, he leaned back in his chair and stretched his long legs. "Some are actually happy."

"Easy for a confirmed bachelor like you to say." Danny snorted. "Name me one happy marriage, one that lasted and didn't end badly?" He hated the bitterness in his voice, hated the despair and the disillusionment he felt.

Peter's smile widened. "Your parents', my parents', your grandfather's, and my grandfather's." Absently, Peter stroked the glass dome that held a place of honor on his desk. Inside was an antique pocket watch. It had belonged to his grandfather, brought from Ireland on that long-ago day when he'd sailed to America to join his brother, Daniel, to seek his fortune and his love.

The pocket watch had belonged to his grandfather's grandfather, and had been passed down from generation to generation. It had been given to his father on the day of his wedding to his mother, and now sat on his desk, as the oldest son, to be passed down to the first of his kin who married. Since neither he nor his two brothers had any intention of getting married anytime soon, he figured the watch would be a permanent fixture on his desk.

At least for the time being.

He stroked the clear, domed glass, then looked at Danny. "The Sullivan men have a history of long, happy marriages. What happened to you was…unfortunate, but I don't think it should make you bitter about marriage."

"I'm not bitter," Danny protested, knowing it was a lie. He was bitter, and it shamed him, for he knew what a joy and blessing a long, happy, loving marriage could be to a man. And a woman.

The *right* woman.

"Then think about what I said, Danny. If you were married, this situation with Molly would be a whole lot easier. An abandoned child is automatically placed with DCFS, and then a foster home. It's standard procedure. Like I said, they look for a nuclear family. Getting married would immediately make you and Katie a nuclear family and definitely give us a leg up. Might even make an adoption easier once we locate the birth mother." He looked at Danny. "So what do you think?"

What Peter had said made a lot of sense, to his mind. It was his heart that was giving him trouble.

"I'll think about it," Danny promised, glancing at his watch. "Keep me posted, Peter. I've got to go."

"By the way, how's Martha?"

Danny stopped in his tracks and turned to his cousin in surprise. "How in the heck did you know about Martha?"

Peter shrugged, amused. "We do legal work for the shelter. Pro bono," he added before Danny could ask. "Tell her I said hello."

"I will."

"By the way, Danny. Great shoes."

Automatically, Danny glanced at his feet, making Peter laugh. "Not yours, Danny. Martha's."

With a wave, Danny headed out the door, his heart heavy, his mind reeling.

"Katie?"

"In here."

Carrying a bag of groceries, Danny wandered through

the playroom and into the kitchen, grinning as he spotted Katie sitting on the floor with Molly, up to her eyeballs in bright-colored toys.

"How are my girls?" he asked, bending to plant a smacking kiss on Molly's cheek and one on top of Katie's head. Molly beamed, giggling and gurgling at the sight of him.

"We're fine," Katie announced with a smile, rattling a bright plastic toy in front of Molly's hands until the baby closed her fingers around it and clumsily drew it to her mouth, sucking greedily. "We've been working on her gross and small motor skills today. And she's doing wonderfully, aren't you, love?"

"I see," he said with a frown, not seeing anything of the kind. "Isn't she a little young to be tinkering around with motors?" he asked as he set the bag of groceries on the counter and began unpacking them.

She laughed. "Not those kind of motors, Danny. This has to do with things like eye-hand coordination, balance, grip—things like that."

He stared at her in admiration. Her devotion to Molly was unbelievable. "You never fail to amaze me, Katie." He shook his head, realizing it was true. "Just when I think I know everything about you, you come up with some surprise."

She flushed, pleased by the compliment. "Thank you. I think." She glanced at the bag. "What's for dinner?"

He grinned. In the past month, they'd worked out a system. Since she spent most of the day taking care of an assortment of kids, he spent the evening taking care of her and Molly. He thought it was an even exchange. Once they had dinner together, either at the center or at her apartment, they settled Molly down for the night, then enjoyed the rest of the evening together, doing nothing more exciting than talking, or watching TV or movies. He never realized how much fun just doing simple things could be when you were with someone who made you happy.

"Reservations," he said with a wicked grin. He finished putting away the groceries, then folded the bag. "I thought for a change we'd go out tonight. Now before you say it, Ma and Da offered to baby-sit. Actually, they almost started a war with Joanna and Michael over who would take care of Molly tonight."

"What's the occasion?" she asked, suddenly suspicious.

He shrugged. "I thought you might enjoy a night out." He didn't add that since she'd been granted temporary custody of Molly, she hadn't left the baby's side except to go to the grocery store or run errands. A night out would be a much-needed change of pace.

"What else?" she asked with a lift of her brow. "I know you too well, Danny. You've got that worry line between your brow." Gathering Molly, she got to her feet, her heart thrumming in trepidation. "What's going on?"

He sighed. He should have known she would spot his worry. Hiding his moods from Katie was like trying to hide an elephant on the monkey bars.

"I stopped to see Peter today."

"And?" Her heart began to beat wickedly. She knew time was running out, knew, too, that she had no idea what she would do if she had to give up Molly. She couldn't bear the thought. She simply couldn't bear it.

He laid a gentle hand on her cheek. "I'll tell you at dinner."

The restaurant was a surprise. She'd expected a noisy café or a cop's hangout. Barrigan's was neither. It was a quiet, elegant steak house on the North Shore that boasted cozy tables, intimate lighting and food to die for.

As they sipped drinks in the small, intimate bar while they waited for their table, Katie brought Danny up to date on her day. It had become habit that they discussed their day with each other, offering sympathy, seeking advice, sharing experiences. A habit she'd come to enjoy immensely. She hadn't realized how happy just sharing little things could make her.

"Martha and Mrs. Hennypenny have decided to take a weekend and go to Las Vegas," Katie said as they were seated at their table.

He almost choked on his drink. "What?" If she'd told him Martha had decided to swim the Atlantic, he couldn't have been more surprised.

Katie laughed, reaching out to touch his hand in a gesture that was so natural she hadn't realized she was doing it until Danny's fingers, warm and tender, closed over hers, sending her pulse fluttering, as his touch always did.

"You haven't heard the best part," she added with a smile. Soft amber lights flickered over Danny's face, bathing it in shadows. He was so handsome he took her breath away.

The past month had been the happiest of her life. There had always been a bond between them, but now that bond had grown and strengthened.

Where once she had given up hope of ever having him see her or love her as a woman, hope now sprung anew. When he looked at her, she could almost see the love in his eyes. She wondered how long it would take him to realize what she already knew.

He loved her.

Not as a kid, or a sister, or a member of the family. But as a woman.

She'd been hugging the knowledge to her heart like a rare and precious secret. She'd waited her whole life for Danny to look at her the way he did now.

It would take some time for him to accept his true feelings, she realized, knowing he would fight it, but she'd waited a lifetime for him. She could be patient and wait a little longer. She would wait as long as it took. He was worth it, and what they could have together would be worth it. The past month had given her a glimpse of what their life could be like together, and it was better than all of her dreams, but then reality always was.

"Martha going to Las Vegas for the weekend isn't the best part?" he asked skeptically, trying not to laugh.

The past month had brought dramatic changes to Martha's life, compliments of Katie. She'd given Martha a job at the center as Mrs. Hennypenny's assistant, and Martha and Mrs. Hennypenny had become instant friends. Before the first week was out, Mrs. Hennypenny had moved Martha into her spare bedroom, claiming her house was too big and lonely for her and she welcomed the company.

Danny had watched mesmerized as Martha metamorphosed. Katie had taken her shopping and helped pick out a new wardrobe for her, then taken her to the beauty salon for a new style and cut. The old Martha was gone—except for her snazzy red shoes, which she adamantly refused to give up.

"Nope." Katie grinned, sipping her drink with her free hand. "They've decided to go to Las Vegas...on a singles' weekend."

"A singles' weekend?" he asked perplexed, then his eyes widened. "You mean Martha and Mrs. Hennypenny are going to Las Vegas to look for...men?"

She laughed at his outraged expression. "Yes, Danny. To look for men. Just because they've reached a certain age doesn't mean they're not interested in love and romance any longer." Her eyes went dreamy. "Love can happen at any age."

"Yeah, but—"

"And," she added wickedly, giving him a smug smile. "They're taking your mom with them."

This time he did choke, nearly spitting his beer across three tables.

Laughing, she slapped him hard on the back.

"My *mother?*" he croaked, grabbing a glass of water and choking it down. "What on earth is my mother doing going on a singles' weekend to Sin City?" His eyes narrowed as visions of loud, leering men in plaid polyester danced in his head. "Does Da know about this?"

Katie laughed, giving his hand a little squeeze. "It was his idea."

Danny groaned. He should have known. "He probably

just suggested it so he could have a weekend alone to smoke his beloved cigars in peace.''

''Or maybe he just wanted a little time to romance the Widow O'Bannion without the whole family breathing down his neck.''

''Da?'' Danny shook his head. What on earth was going on? Was the whole world going nuts? Or just his family? Joanna was having not one, not two, but three babies, and Michael was sporting more gray hairs by the day. His mother was going off on a singles' weekend to Las Vegas to…to—he couldn't even bear to think about it. And Da was going to do the two-step with Mrs. O'Bannion.

''Don't look so shell-shocked, Danny.'' She couldn't help but laugh at the look on his face. ''You may look at them as family, but they're still people with feelings, needs and desires.''

He groaned. ''I don't think I want to be talking about my mother's or Da's needs or desires.''

Laughing, she squeezed his hand again. She'd deliberately avoided asking about his meeting with Peter earlier that afternoon. She'd wanted to give him a chance to relax first.

''So tell me, how was your day?''

He shrugged. ''Pretty average.''

Carefully, she circled the rim of her glass with the tip of her finger. ''Do you want to tell me about your meeting with Peter?''

He glanced away for a moment. She was sitting so close, looking so beautiful, that suddenly he felt like a fifteen-year-old on his first date. His hands itched to touch her, to stroke the long length of her hair, to caress the ivory creaminess of her cheek, to run his thumb along the softness of her lower lip. Looking at her made him realize how much he wanted her.

And he knew better than to want something he couldn't have.

''Danny?'' she prompted softly, cupping his chin and

turning him toward her. Their eyes met and she felt her heart do an unexpected roll.

"We've only got three more days to find Molly's birth mother," he said softly.

"Peter's investigators haven't learned anything?" she asked worriedly.

He shook his head. "Nope. Nothing. They're going to keep working on it, but Peter's not very hopeful."

Tears swam in her eyes. She couldn't help it. "We're going to lose Molly, aren't we?"

His jaw tightened and his expression grew grim. He slid his arm around her and drew her closer. Her scent tickled his senses, distracting him, and it took some effort to keep his mind on what he was saying. "Not if I can help it." He couldn't even bear to entertain the thought. "At the end of the thirty days, Peter said we could petition the courts to appoint one of us as Molly's permanent foster parent—"

"But?" She knew there was a but; she could see the worry in his eyes.

He sighed, then sipped his drink. He'd been thinking about this all afternoon, had in fact thought of nothing else, and he'd come up with what he thought was the most logical solution. "But the fact of the matter is the courts aren't keen on appointing single people as foster parents, not when there might be a two-parent family who could take a child."

Her temper bristled. "That's ridiculous, Danny. More than fifty percent of all children are raised in single-parent homes."

"Yes, but those are natural parents, Katie. When you're dealing with the court system, they have a tendency to want things nice and tidy and by the book."

Fear clutched her heart. "What are we going to do, Danny?"

"Well," he began slowly, closing his hand more tightly over hers. "I think I've come up with a practical plan that just might solve our problem."

Her heart leapt in anticipation. They'd spent hours and

hours talking over every angle they could think of this past month. It was hard to believe that Danny had come up with something new, something they hadn't yet thought of.

"What?" Her gaze searched his and she noted that he shifted uncomfortably.

"We…could get married, Katie."

She stared at him in shock. It was the last thing in the world she'd expected him to say.

"Now hear me out before you object." He'd spent the afternoon rehearsing what he would say. "You love Molly and I love Molly. She needs two parents, and we quite coincidentally fit the bill." He grinned, wondering why Katie had gone so pale. "So if we get married, we'd have a much better chance of gaining temporary custody of Molly as foster parents, and from a legal standpoint we'd be in a much better position to adopt her once we locate her mother." He paused to sip his beer, wondering why his mouth had gone dry as a desert. "It's really the most practical thing to do."

"Practical," she repeated dully. It took an effort for her to get breath in and out of her lungs. Her stomach had begun lurching, as if she was swaying on the deck of a ship.

She'd waited her whole life to hear these words from Danny. To hear him ask her to marry him, to spend her life with him. Now they rung hollowly in her ears as she tried to swallow her tears and the lump that had formed in her throat. Her drink tasted bitter on her tongue.

Practical, she thought again as the word nearly burned her brain. How dare he reduce what she felt for him, what they had, what they'd gone through to something… practical. With great effort, she hung on to her patience and her temper.

"Danny," she said slowly. "Did it ever occur to you that I might not want to marry you?" Just saying the words nearly broke her heart, or what was left of it after he had just broken it. Having Danny as her husband was all she'd ever wanted, but not like this, never like this. Not because it was…practical.

He looked as if she'd sucker punched him. "What do you mean, you might not want to marry me?" Irish pride warred with anger. He didn't know if he was more insulted or offended. "Why on earth wouldn't you want to marry me?" he asked, totally perplexed. "You know me better than anyone else. We get along great. We've already lived together for half our lives so it's not like either of us is in for any surprises, and we both love Molly. So what's the problem?"

He was, she realized sadly as the flicker of hope that had blossomed in her heart the past month died, snuffed out by his words.

"Danny, why do you want to marry me?" Her gaze met his, and if he noticed the storm brewing in her eyes, he didn't show it.

"Are you hard-of-hearing tonight, or what?" He tugged on a curl of her hair, noting she didn't smile as she usually did. "I thought I just told you why I thought we should get married."

"Because it's…practical?"

"Well, yeah…I guess." He was beginning to get the feeling something was wrong. What, he wasn't certain.

"You want me to marry you in order to give Molly two parents who love her, is that right?"

That wasn't quite all he'd meant, but it was close enough. He shrugged, then sipped his drink. "Yeah, I guess that's about right."

"I see," she said quietly. "Danny, did it ever occur to you that marriage is a serious business, not to be taken lightly?"

He sobered instantly. "I'm the last person in the world you have to remind of that, Katie. Believe me." He took a long sip of his beer. "That's why this is perfect for everyone concerned."

"Excuse me?" Her tone was cold enough to chill his drink.

"You know about Carla, and how I feel about emotional entanglements. They're not for me, not ever again. This is the best possible solution. A marriage with no emotional complications, no risks." No chance of getting hurt.

"I see." And she was heartily afraid she did. All too clearly. "Do you realize," she said slowly, lifting her stricken gaze to his, "that you're making the same mistake all over again?"

He frowned, instantly defensive. "What are you talking about?"

"This is just like your marriage to Carla."

Stunned, he stared at her slack jawed. "This is *nothing* like my marriage to Carla. Nothing at all." His teeth clenched until they hurt. How could she even equate what they had to him and Carla? It was almost a mockery. The things he felt for Katie went deeper than anything he'd ever felt for *anyone*. But he couldn't tell her that, it would make him far too vulnerable.

"It's exactly like your marriage to Carla," she countered insistently. "You've asked a woman to marry you because of a baby."

His mouth snapped shut as realization hit him. Until this moment, he'd been oblivious to the tension throbbing in the air. Now it pulsed around him, making his guts tense. "But, Katie, it's not like…" His voice trailed off as he realized maybe what she was saying had a grain of truth to it, and he wasn't certain he liked what he was hearing.

Katie took a deep breath, swallowing the lump in her throat and blinking away hot tears. Danny wasn't the only one with a strong dose of Irish pride. "Danny, I have something to say to you, and I want you to listen to me very, very carefully." She prayed for the courage to get through this without crying. Or killing him.

"I have loved you my entire life—"

"Hey, Kat, you know I love you, too. That goes without saying." Studying her intently, he sipped his beer.

She tightened her fingers on her glass instead of around his neck. "Danny, you're not hearing me." Her voice sounded strained even to her own ears. Taking a deep breath, she prayed for patience, wondering how he could be such a blockhead, wondering how she could go on, knowing her heart was breaking.

"I know you love me, Danny, but there is a big difference between loving someone and being *in love* with them." Tears threatened, but she forced them back. "I'm *in love* with you, Danny, and I have been for most of my life, but you've been too blind or too stupid to see it." She ignored the look on his face and the tears pooling in her eyes. "When I decided to come home, I made a promise to myself. If I couldn't get you to see me as a woman and love me the same way I loved you, then I would simply have to get on with my life...with someone else."

"What are you saying, Katie?" He didn't want to hear this, didn't want to know that she was thinking of spending her life with someone other than him. Pain sliced through him, leaving him open, exposed. Nothing had ever hurt this much.

"What I'm saying, Danny, is that I've finally realized how futile this all is." Impotently, she waved her arm in the air. "I realize now that you are never going to love me the way I love you, and even if you could, you'd never accept it because you're afraid."

"Katie—"

"No." She held up her hand, fearing she would break down if he didn't let her finish. "Please, hear me out. I love Molly more than anything in the world, and I agree that she needs two parents, but that doesn't mean we have to be married. Thousands of children grow up in households where their parents aren't married. As long as we love her, what difference is a marriage license going to make? That little piece of paper would be worthless. It wouldn't mean anything. Not to you. Not to me. Not to anyone, not under these circumstances. And a marriage license isn't going to make either of us love her any more or any less."

"Katie, I don't understand." He shook his head. He

thought he'd found the perfect solution. A way to adopt Molly, and keep Katie in his life without either of them getting hurt or being vulnerable. Now, he realized how foolish he'd been. Foolish to reduce what they had to a practical arrangement.

"I'm not going to marry you, Danny. Not now. Not ever." Her voice rang out strong and proud in the quiet restaurant. "Not for Molly's sake, and definitely *not* to be practical. Marriage is far too sacred to me to do something like that." She shot to her feet, ignoring the interested looks of the other diners. Her chin lifted.

"The man I marry is going to love me, Danny—for *me*. Because he wants to share his life and his love with me, and not for any other reason. I won't settle for anything less." She dropped her napkin to the table. "I was willing to offer you everything I had—my life, my love—and all you can offer in return is your name. Not your love. You're never going to give that. I understand that now." Her voice nearly broke. Tears blurred her eyes, but she dashed them away with trembling hands. She refused to break down in front of him. "I appreciate your offer, Danny, but I can't accept." She turned on her heel, wanting to flee before she made more of a fool of herself, but he reached for her arm, stopping her flight.

"Katie, please. What about us?" Panic clutched his heart, his soul, but he didn't know how to stop it, how to turn things around, how to make her understand.

She sniffled. "There is no *us*, Danny. There never has been and there never will be because you're too afraid to love. And I value myself too much to accept a marriage to a man who can't love me." She swallowed past the lump that now felt like a boulder. "Unless it pertains to Molly's care, I don't want to see you." She couldn't face him any longer, not knowing how things were. He'd stripped her of all hope and broken her heart. She had to accept they would never be together. And go on.

"Katie, come on, you can't be serious." The idea of not being able to see her, to talk to her, to be with her, was so frightening he felt a chill skip up his spine. Already he felt the loss all the way to his soul. "Please stay, we'll talk about this." He had no idea how to change what he'd just done. He'd hurt her, he realized dully, surprised at the shaft of pain it caused in his own heart. He'd hurt Katie, something he'd never wanted to do. He hadn't meant it; he was merely trying to protect himself. But in doing so, he'd hurt her, and he knew that would be harder to live with.

She shook her head. "There's nothing left to talk about. You've said everything I care to hear." She glanced down at his hand, still encircling her arm. "Let me go," she whispered. She couldn't bear having him touch her, knowing he would never touch her the way a man touched the woman he loved. "Please, Danny. Just let me go."

It was the sound of her voice, so soft, so sad, so…broken, that had him releasing her, and cursing himself. Helpless, he watched her flee the restaurant, wondering why his heart was aching so badly.

"Your Honor, if it pleases the court, we'd like to present a letter from her birth mother verifying her identity." Peter stepped toward the judge's bench and passed over the papers.

In a fluke of luck the shelter had received an envelope with a note from Molly's birth mother, explaining the circumstances of her abandonment of Molly. Not knowing what to do with the material, the director of the shelter had called Peter for legal advice. It had been the break they'd been waiting for.

"As you can see, Your Honor, the birth mother unfortunately passed away within twenty-four hours of abandoning her child at the shelter. Since that time, the child has been in the care and custody of my client. At this time, I would like to petition the court to grant permanent custody of the child known as Molly Doe to Katie Wagner as a foster parent, pending formal legal proceedings toward adoption. I believe I've already explained the extenuating circumstances to the court, and would be happy to answer any further questions the court might have.''

Perusing the material, the judge nodded thoughtfully, then glanced up at Peter, Katie and Danny. ''Yes, I'm well aware of the circumstances, Mr. Sullivan. Unusual as they are.'' The judge glanced at Katie again. ''And do you believe, Ms. Wagner, that you are fully capable to raise this child in a competent manner, even though you are single and have a vested interest in a business that requires an enormous amount of your time?''

Katie stepped forward, holding Molly in her arms, not liking the scowl on the judge's face. ''Your Honor, I most certainly do. I couldn't love Molly any more if she were my own.'' With a soft smile, she glanced down at the baby. ''I know what it's like to be abandoned. My own parents were killed when I was barely five years old. I was fortunate enough to have been welcomed into another family.'' She glanced at Danny, standing silently beside her, and felt the pain in her heart, raw and fresh, but she couldn't dwell on it now. She had to secure Molly's future, even though her own was in shambles. She looked over her shoulder. The entire Sullivan clan was seated in the gallery, lending their moral support.

''I know what a difference a loving family can make to a child who's lost everything. I know because I've been there.'' Her voice dropped and she fought back tears. ''You feel lost, alone, abandoned, as if there is no place for you in this big world. It seems as if everyone has someone to love, but you. Everyone belongs somewhere but you. Fortunately, I was adopted by a wonderful family. The Sullivans raised me as their own, even though there was no blood between us—even when Maeve Sullivan became a single parent. They taught me how valuable a family is, and that blood doesn't make a family—love does.'' She glanced back at her Aunt Maeve and Da, and saw tears in their eyes.

''I want Molly to know what it's like to be surrounded by love, by family. To know that she's wanted and valued.

To understand that she'll always have a place in this world, a place that has nothing to do with who gave birth to her, but who raised and loved her.'' Head high, eyes shimmering with tears, she took another step closer. "Giving birth doesn't make you a mother, Your Honor. It's the day-in-day-out care and attention you give a child that makes someone a mother. It's pacing the floor all night, sick with worry because your child is feverish. It's staying up half the night, sewing a Halloween costume for a school play. It's watching 'Sesame Street' until your eyes are bleary and you're nearly deaf. It's making macaroni and cheese every day for a week simply because it's all your child will eat.'' She laughed through her tears, reminiscing about some of the things she'd put her Aunt Maeve through over the years. "It's giving a child your heart and your love, knowing that there's nothing else in the world that's as important.''

She took a long, slow breath, then continued. "Da Sullivan once told me that the most important job a person can have is raising a child. In a hundred years it won't matter how much money you made or how many promotions you got. But if you raised and cared for a child, if you made a difference in another human being's life, then you've contributed something worthwhile to this life. And I agree with him wholeheartedly.'' Chin lifted, she blinked away her tears. "Your Honor, I'm asking you to please give me the chance to make a difference in Molly's life. To give her all the things I was fortunate to receive as I was growing up. To let me help her become the best woman—the best person—she can be. I know that I can do that, with your permission, of course.'' Katie stepped back, unaware that she'd moved closer to the judge's bench.

"Come here, young lady,'' the judge ordered softly.

Katie cast a frantic glance at Peter, wondering what she'd done. He nodded and she stepped up to the bench.

The judge stood, then came down the steps and around the bench. "Let me have a look at this child.''

She handed Molly to him, amazed at how his weathered face broke into wrinkly smiles. "She's a lucky young lady,

Ms. Wagner." His gaze met Katie's and her heart soared. "Very lucky, indeed." He brushed his hand across the top of Molly's hand for a moment as she tried to grab the glasses that were hanging around his neck, then handed the baby back to her.

Katie snuggled Molly closer and waited breathlessly for his decision.

Once seated, the judge cleared his throat. "In spite of the unusual circumstances—or rather because of them, Ms. Wagner—I am going to grant custody of this child to you. But you must abide by all the rules and regulations required of the state."

"Of course." Her heart was so full she thought it might burst. She glanced at Danny and could see the relief on his face, as well. But there was something else there, something she couldn't recognize.

The judge banged his gavel. "Well, Ms. Wager." He smiled. "Congratulations. I believe you've just become a mother."

Laughing through her tears, Katie endured hugs from everyone—everyone, that is, except Danny, who stood staring at her, looking lost, looking alone. Without a word to anyone, he walked out of the courtroom.

Chapter Ten

Danny was miserable.

It had been almost a month since he'd walked out of that courtroom. Almost a month since Katie had moved back to the Sullivan home to give him full access to Molly, and to give Molly the benefit of their full extended, loving family. Katie still wouldn't see him or talk to him, unless it pertained to Molly. She was cool, polite and so damn distant he wanted to shake her.

She kept Molly at the center during the day, where the baby was spoiled and fussed over by Katie, Martha and Mrs. Hennypenny. He stopped every day to see Molly, usually on his lunch hour or when he was in the neighborhood. Katie never objected and, in fact, seemed to welcome him, but she wouldn't talk to him about anything but Molly.

In the evening, when Katie came home with Molly in tow, it was a fight to see who would get to spend time with Molly. He and Katie truly had joint custody since they were both a big part of her everyday life, yet not a part of each other's.

And he was still miserable.

If the family was aware of the growing tensions between

them, no one said anything—at least not to him. But then, he had been about as sociable as a sick bear, growling at everyone who dared venture into his path.

The weekends were the hardest. He didn't have work to occupy his time, and so he spent endless hours alone, brooding about what a mess he'd made of things. Of his life. Of his relationship with Katie.

This weekend had been particularly hard. His mother had gone to Las Vegas with Mrs. Hennypenny and Martha. Joanna and Michael had taken little Emma and Molly to Lake Geneva, and Patrick had taken himself off somewhere, leaving Danny alone, and feeling incredibly lonely.

He thought of going out, but couldn't seem to drum up enough energy, knowing Katie was just down the hall, and there were more than just walls between them.

So he spent the weekend prowling around his apartment. By Sunday afternoon, he'd nearly worn the soles off his shoes.

Katie had been right, he realized miserably.

He'd been afraid. Afraid of admitting how he really felt about her. Afraid to admit that he'd fallen in love with her.

Just as he'd done when he lost his child, he'd buried his feelings, not wanting to face or accept them.

How could he have been such a blind fool?

He'd wasted so much time, taking Katie for granted, assuming she would always be there for him.

It wasn't until he'd lost her that he realized how much he needed her, loved her.

Not as a sister, not even as a mother for Molly, but as a woman, as his wife. The woman who was meant for him. His soul mate, his other half.

It was just as his mother had told him. If he'd listened to his heart instead of blocking out what he didn't want to face, he would have known before he made a complete mess of things.

A knock at the door had him growling. He didn't want to see anyone, didn't want to talk to anyone—except Katie. But he knew darn well it wasn't her at the door.

Whether he wanted company or not, the door burst open. "Ah, Danny Boy, so what's it you're doing up here that's worrying me so?" Unmindful of the glare his grandson sent toward him, Da stepped into the apartment and over the clutter of clothes and debris collected over the weekend, and shut the door softly behind him.

"Da, I'm fine," he said, dragging a hand through his hair.

"Aye, I can see that, lad." Cocking his head, Da inspected his grandson with wise eyes, remembering a similar conversation he'd had with Michael not so long ago. These grandsons of his could be stubborn cusses. It made him proud. "You're just fine. I can see that. Three days' worth of beard. No shower for longer than that. You growling at the door like some wounded cub. Fine you are, son." Da nodded sagely. "Aye, I can see that with my own eyes."

"Da—"

"Danny Boy, let me tell you a story." Da paused, choosing his words carefully as he dropped an affectionate arm around his grandson, his own heart aching for the boy's pain. "We men, sometimes we make a wee bit of a mess of things. Especially with the women in our lives." Da stroked his jaw thoughtfully. "It can't be helped, son. I guess it's the nature of the beast. We think that it's a sin to show our feelings, to show we care, or that we love, or that we're afraid." Laughing at Danny's expression, Da drew back. "Now don't be looking at me like I'm daft, son. I know of what I speak. I made a wee bit of a mess of things a time or two in my day. But your beloved grandmother taught me something very important right before she left my side."

At the mention of his grandmother, Danny glanced up at his grandfather curiously, hearing the pain in the old man's voice.

"What, Da?"

Satisfied he finally had his grandson's attention, Da continued. "When I first laid eyes on your lovely grandmother, Danny Boy, she was just a wee bit of a thing and pretty as a picture. Lord have mercy, she made my mouth go dry just to look at her.'' His eyes misted as his voice grew wistful. ''Whenever she was near, I'd feel as if someone had tied my tongue into knots. It was just that I was so in awe of her, and of what she made me feel.'' He shuddered involuntarily, still stung by the punch that had never faded, not even after all these years. ''She thought I didn't care for her, son, because I never said my feelings. I never told her how she moved me, or how I felt when she looked at me, or how I longed to hold her in my arms. I was afraid, son, afraid of the power of what I felt, afraid to look foolish, afraid that she'd laugh, but more afraid than anything that she wouldn't return my feelings.'' Da sighed, drawing his arm around Danny and bringing him closer. ''She told me something right before she passed on to a better place, something I never forgot.''

''What, Da?''

Da smiled, his eyes still wistful. ''She told me that a woman needs to hear the words, son, the words of what fills a man's heart. How is she ever to know what's in his heart if he never speaks of it? She said if a man fears what he feels, then what he feels is far deeper than his fear.''

''That's it?'' Danny asked, puzzled.

Da laughed. ''You see, son. We men, sometimes we're such a thickheaded lot. What's worse to fear than losing the woman you love? A woman who moves your heart and lifts your spirit? A woman like that comes along but once in a lifetime, Danny Boy, and a wise man doesn't let her go.''

''I've made a mess of things with Katie,'' Danny reluctantly admitted.

''Aye, son, I know that,'' Da said with a laugh. ''And so does everyone in the family. We love you both. It would be hard not to see there's tension between you.''

''She said she wouldn't marry me.''

''Any particular reason why she should marry you?'' Da asked with a smile, startling Danny.

''Because I love her, Da.'' He dragged a hand through

his mussed hair. "I've been in love with her for a long time. I guess I was just too...afraid to admit it."

"I see." Da looked thoughtful. "And have you told her this, son?"

Danny shook his head. "No, Da."

"Aye," Da said with a sigh. Eyes twinkling, he glanced up to the heavens. "And the boy wonders why she won't marry him?" He shook his head in dismay.

"She won't see me or talk to me, not unless it pertains to Molly."

"Posh, boy! We Sullivan men have been fighting for the women we love for more years than I can recall. Are you telling me that my grandson is going to let a little something like...silence keep him from the woman he loves?" Not if he knew his grandson. Pride had its place, he realized with an inward smile. And, like him, Danny had been blessed with an abundance of it.

"Da, do you think—"

Da poked him in the chest. "That's the problem, Danny Boy, you think too much. What we need here, laddie, is a little action." Da rocked back on his heels and watched his grandson. "Unless, of course, you're a...coward." They were fighting words, he knew, but something strong was needed here.

Danny needed no further prodding. He knew what he had to do. He turned and headed toward the door, only to have Da lay a gentle hand on his arm, stopping him.

"Son." Eyes twinkling, Da wrinkled his nose. "Three days it's been, lad, and I think a wee bit of a shower and a shave might be in order first. A clean set of clothes might not be a bad idea, as well." Laughing, Da shook his head as Danny bolted toward the shower, grateful he had only Patrick left to marry.

Unless, of course... Da sat down in a chair and began planning. A wide grin claimed his mouth. Three boys, Jo-anna had said. Three, proud strapping Sullivan grandsons were soon to be born to carry on the Sullivan name and tradition. His heart swelled with pride. A new generation of Sullivans. Three more Sullivan brothers to love, to watch grow and prosper and, with any luck, fall in love.

Aye, it was going to be a fine time ahead.

Da rubbed his stubbled chin. Perhaps he'd better lay in a hefty supply of cigars.

Katie was miserable. Unable to bear being cooped up in her apartment, she'd come down to the center, hoping to keep herself occupied, her thoughts off Danny.

It had been hard getting on with her life, facing each day knowing that Danny would never be a part of her life again—at least, not in the way she'd always hoped.

With a sigh, she pushed a wad of hair off her forehead, then continued unloading the groceries she'd bought for the center for the upcoming week. She'd already cleaned every corner and crevice twice, so now there was little left to do but stock the refrigerator.

It was almost dusk, and she'd been working all day. But the physical activity helped to exhaust her so she could get some sleep at night. Nights were the hardest, when her dreams tormented her, and her tears fell hot and heavy.

If it wasn't for Molly, she didn't know what she would do. She wondered if Danny knew Molly was getting her first tooth. The thought brought a spate of fresh tears. He should be here, she thought, alongside her, sharing her life and Molly's, but it was never to be, and wishing wouldn't make it so.

A gentle knock at the back door had her brows drawing together in a frown. It was almost seven. Who could be knocking at the center door?

Leaving her groceries, she went to the back door and peeked out the window. There was no one there. Puzzled, she turned and headed back to the kitchen when the knock sounded again. Growing annoyed, she turned and looked out the window, but again, no one was there.

Thinking it was neighborhood kids pulling a prank, she unlocked the dead bolt and stepped outside, determined to put a stop to this nonsense.

The alley was empty.

It was almost July now, and the air had turned hot and heavy, pressing in like a thick, wet blanket. Paper and debris swirled around her feet, swept up by the faint hint of a breeze that managed to sneak past the heavy air. The full darkness had not descended yet, but the sky was an eerie shade of orange, casting a hazy pallor over everything.

In spite of the warmth of the day, Katie felt a shiver pass over her. Except for a few abandoned cars scattered about at each end of the alley, it was deserted. Unsettled and not knowing why, she glanced around.

Annoyed at herself for feeling so skittish, she turned to go back inside when a hand landed heavily on her shoulder, causing her to let loose a screech.

Instinct had her whirling, her heart pounding in unadulterated fear. She didn't think, she merely reacted. Hands clenched, her closed fist connected with something solid and hard.

"Dammit." The breath whooshed out of him and he doubled over.

"Danny?" Her heart tumbled over in her chest, and she hesitantly took a step closer, laying a comforting hand on his back. "Danny?" she said again. Her pulse began a mad scramble and she was almost certain her knees were going to buckle.

"Good Lord, Kat," he huffed, blowing out a breath and trying to ease the pain in his gut. "We're going to have to sign you up as a professional pretty soon."

Relief, anguish and anger surged through her and she nervously wiped her hands down her jeans.

"What are you doing here, Danny?" She tried to make her voice cold and impersonal, but she failed miserably as her eyes drank him in. It was so good to see him. In spite of his labored breathing and doubled-over stance, he looked wonderful. Her heart ached anew.

"I brought you something." He grunted, straightening. His gaze met hers and he saw the impact the past month had had. Dark circles underscored her beautiful doe eyes, and she looked as if she'd lost weight. She probably hadn't been eating properly, he realized with a hint of worry. He wanted to grab her and haul her into his arms and tell her she was right, that he had been an idiot, but he couldn't. Not yet. He had other things to do first.

"You brought me something?" she asked suspiciously. She remembered the last time he'd brought her something, and scowled. "It better be the mumps this time, Danny, because I guarantee you I'm not in the mood for much else."

"Nope." He grinned, leaning against the building and tucking his hands in his pockets so he wouldn't touch her. He knew he probably had one shot, and he wasn't about to blow it, not this time. "Not the mumps. This time it's actually a present." He frowned. "Well, it's sort of a present."

She looked at him skeptically. "Sort of a present?" She shouldn't be talking to him. She should just turn around and march into the center and shut the door in his face. He deserved no less. But she didn't move.

"And is this particular present soft and cuddly?" she asked, thinking of Molly.

"No. Actually it's cold, hard and not something I'd recommend for cuddling."

Interest piqued in spite of herself, Katie lifted her chin. "I'm not talking to you," she announced, despite the fact that she was doing exactly that. "And I'm not interested in your presents." She turned to go, but he snagged her arm with two gentle fingers, making her heart tumble over in her chest.

"Kat, please." The pleading tone in his voice made her look at him. "At least hear me out." He didn't wait for an answer. He reached in his pocket and extracted a little black velvet box and handed it to her. Her eyes widened for a fraction of a moment. She recognized the box. It had sat on Da's dresser for as long as she could remember.

"What is that, Danny?" She had to swallow hard to get

the words out. Just being near him made her heart ache, and her arms long to hold him.

"Your present," he said softly, drawing her close in spite of her stiffness, and lifting her hand to his lips for a kiss. "Open it."

She did, slowly. The small gold hinges on the velvet case creaked softly as she opened the lid. Her breath caught and her gaze flew to his in total confusion. "Danny...this...this is—"

"My grandmother's engagement ring," he finished for her. A family heirloom, it was this ring that had started the circle of love and tradition that meant everything to the Sullivans. "Da gave it to her the night they fled Ireland."

"I know," Katie whispered, tears filling her eyes. She remembered sitting on the floor, listening in awe as Da told the story. Romantic to a fault, she would ask him to repeat it over and over until tears were streaming down her face. To have a man love you the way Da had loved his wife was a miracle few women would ever know.

Sniffling, she pushed the ring back toward Danny. "I told you. I won't marry you."

"No, Kat. What you said is you wouldn't marry me for Molly's sake. And I'm glad, because I want the woman I'm in love with to marry me because she loves me and only me, and wants to spend her life with me. No other reason will do." He realized now, finally, how much she meant to him. How much he needed her. How much he loved her.

"Danny, we've already been through this. You've made it clear how you feel."

"No, Kat, I don't think I did." Shaking his head, he dragged a hand through his hair. "I couldn't even admit to myself how I felt. You were right." A ghost of a smile played along his mouth. "I was afraid—terrified, in fact— by what I felt for you. I thought I was in love once before, Kat, but now I realize it wasn't love. Hell, I didn't even know what love was until you." He took her hand, drew her closer until he was looking into her eyes. "Marry me,

Kat. Not for Molly's sake, and not for practical reasons, but because I'm in love with you.''

She couldn't speak. Her throat was clogged with tears. She glanced down at the ring, at the small diamond glinting in the fading sun, a ring of permanence, of strength, of love. A ring that had brought together a man and a woman whose love was more powerful than life itself. Her gaze rose to Danny's and she saw the same kind of love in his eyes. Saw the need and the hope and the promise.

It was all she needed to see.

"Yes," she said, whisper soft. "Yes, Danny, I'll marry you."

Danny hesitated. "What about…Sam?"

Laughing, Katie explained, much to Danny's relief, about the crotchety old man.

He hauled her close, closing his eyes, letting his body relax against her, letting her familiar scent engulf him. For the first time in what seemed like a long time he let out a long, deep breath.

His mother was right. There were no doubts, no fears, no worries. There was just joy, peace…happiness, and a completeness he'd never known was possible.

"I love you, Kat." His voice broke, choked by the emotions rising in him. He drew back to look at her. "Can you ever forgive me for being an idiot?"

"Eventually," she said with a laugh, wiping her own tears as she planted kisses across his face.

He pulled the ring out of the box. It flashed and sparkled with a million memories from the past, and the promise of the future. He slipped it on her finger. It fit perfectly. "This was my grandmother's, Kat. Da was saving it for me, for when I met my match."

She frowned, admiring the beautiful ring and the delicate scrolled gold setting. "But why didn't he give it to you when you married—"

He tilted her chin, not letting her finish. "Because he was saving it for when I found my match." He kissed her. "The right match." He grinned, more relieved than he thought possible. "He's a wise old bird, Kat, and somehow he said he always knew. Guess Da and my brothers have had a running bet, wondering how long it would take me to realize you were the woman I was waiting for my whole life." He rested his brow against hers. "Guess I can be a blockhead sometimes."

"You'll get no argument from me," she whispered, throwing her arms around him and holding him close, their hearts beating in unison.

As one, she thought. As it should be.

"I love you, Kat," he whispered. "Let's go home."

Home. It had such a lovely ring to it. Home with Danny. It was where home had been all along.

"Danny?" she whispered as they walked arm and arm back into the center to close up.

"Yeah, hon?" He couldn't let go of her, not yet. Maybe not ever.

"Who won the bet?"

He laughed. "Da. Who else?"

Epilogue

Their wedding was a true Sullivan affair. With the pub filled to the rafters with various Sullivan cousins, nieces, nephews, aunts and uncles, Da gave Katie away, insisting on carrying Molly in his arms while he did. Martha and Mrs. Hennypenny stood up for Katie, while Michael and Patrick stood up for Danny.

And so one fine Saturday morning in July, with the sun shining and the entire family, neighborhood and precinct in attendance, Katie and Danny recited their vows.

Dressed in a simple white silk gown, with a small train and a headpiece of fresh white roses picked from Mrs. Hennypenny's garden, Katie stood with Danny in front of their daughter, their family and their friends and together they pledged their love.

The moment the ceremony was over, the rousing celebration began. Banquet tables were bulging with food, and Maeve had hired an authentic Irish band to play.

"Katie, my girl, it's a fine, fine day for a wedding celebration." Puffing on a large, smelly cigar, Da bent and kissed her cheek, his eyes shining with love, with pride.

"Now you're truly a Sullivan, one of the clan, as it should be."

Carefully, he draped an arm around her shoulder, puffing vigorously on his cigar, blowing a heavy stream of smoke in the air, hoping Maeve wouldn't spot him. He'd been ducking her all afternoon. A man should be able to enjoy a good cigar on the day of his grandson's wedding.

He nodded toward Katie. "You've made me a proud man today, lassie, a proud man, indeed." He lifted her left hand, and looked at the ring that held so many memories. He smiled. "Aye, and your grandmother, bless her soul, would have been proud, as well." He kissed her hand. "She would have loved you, lassie, as much as I." His voice choked, and he hugged Katie tight. He'd loved this child from the moment Maeve and Jock had brought her home. She might not have been family by blood but, aye, she was family in the heart. A far more important place. And he couldn't have been happier that Danny had finally seen the light.

Tears of joy filled Katie's eyes and she hugged Da tight. "I love you, Da," she whispered. "I love you."

He drew back, clearing his throat. "Of course, and why wouldn't you?" he asked, making her laugh.

He glanced across the room to where Molly was sleeping in the Sullivan family cradle. "You've given me another grandchild. And another redheaded girl at that." Beaming, he took another puff and shook his head in wonder. "How lucky can a man be?"

"Honey?" Danny came up next to Katie, sliding his arm around her. He couldn't resist a kiss to her lips. "Molly's fussing. I think that new tooth is bothering her again."

"I'll go to her." She started, but Da reached out a hand to stop her.

"Aye, let me go, lassie. It's time the wee one got to know her great-grandfather." Da started toward the baby, just as Danny reached out and plucked the cigar from his hand.

"She's too young to smoke, Da," Danny scolded, trying not to laugh.

Pulling awkwardly on his cummerbund, Da grumbled something under his breath about ungrateful children as he made his way toward the cradle, which was sitting in a quiet corner of the pub. At the sight of Molly, he grinned. "Aye, there you are, my lassie." He lifted Molly in his arms, cradling the baby close. "Now what's the trouble, love?" He nuzzled her. "Aye, I see the problem. No one's attending to you, is that it?" He chuckled, then sat in an empty seat in a quiet spot of the bar. Holding Molly, Da looked around the room, his eyes drifting to his grandsons, pride swelling his heart.

Mikey, so strong, so proud, and now with a family of his own. He couldn't have been happier.

And Danny, so stubborn and headstrong—and so very much like him, he thought with a laugh. Married now to the woman who was his mate, his match in every way. And with a child of their own.

And then there was Patrick. The baby who was no longer a baby, but a grown man with a whole wide future in front of him. Da laughed, wondering what the future held for Patrick. Mischief, he hoped.

Da glanced down at Molly. Now there was a whole new generation of Sullivans to carry on their name, their tradition. He felt his eyes mist and didn't bother to wipe them. Jock would have been proud of his family, he thought with a smile. Yes, proud, indeed.

Sniffling, Da nuzzled Molly close, then lifted her to look into her beautiful blue eyes. "Sullivan eyes," he said again, convinced. "Aye, it was destined, lassie. Destined, indeed." He shifted her to his arms.

"Now I think it's time you learned about your clan. Ahh, the Sullivan brothers. There were six of us and we were a wild and handsome bunch, lassie." Da glanced at the cradle, and memories of his own youth came flooding back.

"A long, long time ago, one of the Sullivan brothers— and a handsome fellow at that—fell madly in love with a fine and beautiful lass.'' Eyes shining, Da glanced at the baby in his arms and again at the cradle that had carried so many hopes, dreams and memories.

"Well, this pretty little lass was named Molly—'' He grinned suddenly. "Just like you, love, and her hair was as red as yours and her smile just as sweet and charming.'' He sighed heavily, wishing for his cigar. "But alas, Molly, well, she was pledged to another.'' He grinned suddenly, remembering the mayhem that ensued.

"Like I said, lassie, we were the Sullivan brothers, and not known for accepting defeat. So one of the brothers— the one in love with Molly—cooked up a plan. And a fine, grand plan it was,'' Da said with a chuckle of remembrance. "He couldn't bear the thought of his love pledged to another, nor could he accept living his life without her. And so, on the night before her match, when all was quiet, he and his brothers snuck into her camp and stole her.'' Shaking his head, Da laughed as the baby gurgled. "Aye, I knew you'd like this story, love. On that very night, his own brothers helped him spirit his love away from their homeland, and onto a fishing boat that would begin a journey that would take them to their new home. America.'' Da's eyes misted as he thought of that long-ago day. "It was a journey of love and new beginnings. All they had to their name was this cradle, lassie, the one you've been resting in. See, the lad had always known he and his Molly were destined for each other, and he'd made the cradle as a wedding present—something to show his eternal love, and something to pass on to future generations so they would always know of that love.'' His voice grew soft as he stroked the baby's fine, soft red hair.

"They had a wonderful, happy life together, full of mischief and an abundance of love, until the day his Molly girl drew her last breath.'' Sighing softly, Da kissed the baby's soft cheek, holding her close, feeling the ache in his heart. "And, lassie, I'll tell you a secret. It's not a day goes by that I don't miss her.'' Sniffling, he smiled gently, stroking Molly's red hair, so like his own Molly's, as he glanced around at the family he and Molly had created.

"I'm sorry she's not here to see this day, lass. To see our grandson and you, our great-grandchild." Pulling out his hanky, Da swiped at his nose. "Aye, she would have loved you, lassie." He reached out and stroked a hand over the cradle, a cradle he had carved so many years ago with so much love. "I love you, Molly," he whispered, stroking the cradle, and thinking about all the years and the tears and the memories. "Aye, Molly girl, after all these years, I still miss you." He glanced at the baby and smiled. "Aye, you would have been proud."

* * * * *

Don't miss Patrick's story,
BABY AND THE OFFICER,
available in August 1998,
when the last of the Sullivan brothers
finds out what legends—and love—are made of....

AUTHOR'S NOTE

At the time this book was written, the adoption laws stated were legal in the state of Illinois where this story takes place. But since adoption laws vary, please check with your own attorney regarding the adoption laws in your state.

HERE COME THE
Virgin Brides!

*Celebrate the joys of first love with more
unforgettable stories from Romance's
brightest stars:*

SWEET BRIDE OF REVENGE
by Suzanne Carey—June 1998 (SR #1300)

Reader favorite Suzanne Carey weaves a sensuously powerful
tale about a man who forces the daughter of his enemy to be
his bride of revenge. But what happens when this hard-
hearted husband falls head over heels...for his wife?

THE BOUNTY HUNTER'S BRIDE
by Sandra Steffen—July 1998 (SR #1306)

In this provocative page-turner by beloved author
Sandra Steffen, a shotgun wedding is only the beginning when
an injured bounty hunter and the sweet seductress who'd
nursed him to health are discovered in a remote mountain
cabin by her gun-toting dad and *four* brothers!

SUDDENLY...MARRIAGE!
by Marie Ferrarella—August 1998 (SR #1312)

RITA Award-winning author Marie Ferrarella weaves a
magical story set in sultry New Orleans about two people
determined to remain single who exchange vows in a mock
ceremony during Mardi Gras, only to learn their bogus
marriage is the real thing....

*And look for more VIRGIN BRIDES in future months,
only in—*

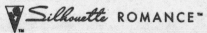

V *Silhouette* ROMANCE™

Available at your favorite retail outlet.

Take 4 bestselling love stories FREE

a FREE surprise gift!

 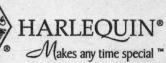

The World's Most Eligible Bachelors are about to be named! And Silhouette Books brings them to you in an all-new, original series....

World's Most Eligible Bachelors

Twelve of the sexiest, most sought-after men share every intimate detail of their lives in twelve never-before-published novels by the genre's top authors.

Don't miss these unforgettable stories by:

Dixie Browning

MARIE FERRARELLA

Jackie Merritt

Tracy Sinclair

BJ James

RACHEL LEE   Suzanne Carey

Gina Wilkins

VICTORIA PADE

MAGGIE SHAYNE   Anne McAllister

Susan Mallery

Look for one new book each month in the
World's Most Eligible Bachelors series beginning
September 1998 from Silhouette Books.

Silhouette®

Available at your favorite retail outlet.

SOMETIMES BIG SURPRISES COME IN SMALL PACKAGES!

Celebrate the happiness that only a baby can bring in Bundles of Joy by Silhouette Romance!

February 1998
On Baby Patrol by Sharon De Vita (SR#1276)

Bachelor cop Michael Sullivan pledged to protect his best friend's pregnant widow, Joanna Grace. Would his secret promise spark a vow to love, honor and cherish? Don't miss this exciting launch of Sharon's *Lullabies and Love* miniseries!

April 1998
Boot Scootin' Secret Baby by Natalie Patrick (SR#1289)

Cowboy Jacob Goodacre discovered his estranged wife, Alyssa, had secretly given birth to his daughter. Could a toddler with a fondness for her daddy's cowboy boots keep her parents' hearts roped together?

June 1998
Man, Wife and Little Wonder by Robin Nicholas (SR#1301)

Reformed bad boy Johnny Tremont would keep his orphaned niece at any price. But could a marriage in name only to pretty Grace Marie Green lead to the love of a lifetime?

And be sure to look for additional BUNDLES OF JOY titles in the months to come.

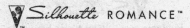

▼ *Silhouette* ROMANCE™

Find us at your favorite retail outlet.